KISSING FROGS : ADULTS ONLY

by James Glachan

JASON'S STORY

JASON had been looking forward to starting his new job and strolled into the dispatch office.

'You are with Charlie, Recycling lorry Number 8,' the dispatcher had said with a sly grin.

Jason's face dropped faster than a man with a palsy. Charlie's run. He had left the Recycling Centre the previous Friday with everybody's best wishes and their hope he wouldn't be assigned to Charlie. The Fates conspired to piss him right off.

So, why not Charlie? His reputation went before him, he

was a grumpy old man. No, the grumpiest. Look up curmudgeon in a Pictionary and it's probably Charlies' picture you would see, he had a face that looked like a bulldog chewing a wasp.

Jason walked to the driver's door of the refuse truck. Standing next to it it seemed big and intimidating. He looked up and saw the dreaded Charlie looking at his paperwork. Charlie wasn't, by reputation, the kind of guy who would take kindly to being disturbed. His nickname among the refuse staff was Shiny, short for Shiny Paper because he took no shit from anybody.

He wanted to disturb him gently, you don't poke a stick at a sleeping rottweiller, he walked round to the front of the wagon, hoping to catch his eye. As he stepped out 5 or 6 feet forward, he was almost knocked down by another lorry making its way out of the yard to start it's run. Feeling defeated, he walked over to the lorry door and knocked on it. Gently at first. The driver either never heard it or ignored it. He knocked again a bit harder next time.

The electric window slid down.

'Keep your wig on. You better not have scratched the paintwork, this wagons brand new.'

Although Charlie spoke he didn't turn his head or venture his head out to see who was knocking.

'Are you Charlie?' Jason said with a tremor in his voice.

'Yip.'

'I'm Jason. I've to come with you. You know, on the round.'

'You better get in quick. I'm about to go off.'

As Jason walked in front of the lorry the engine revved and the big mechanical beast seemed to come alive. For a moment Jason thought it was coming towards him, he nearly shit himself. He ran round, jumped up and opened the passenger door. As he tried to make his ascent Charlie growled at him.

'In the back,' he said and signalled with his thumb- he wasn't allowed in the passenger seat.

Jason stood for a few seconds trying to apprehend what he meant. He looked round and saw another worker in the back. Withdrawing, he got in the back. The occupant leaned forward and stuck out his hand. 'Alan,' he said as a welcome. Jason shook his hand. 'No, it's Jason.'

Alan shook his head perplexed. Was he being landed with an idiot for a mate? 'No, I'm Alan,' he said, pointing to his chest.

Jason took a short time to comprehend. 'Oh, right, I thought you had been told the new guy coming was called Alan. '

Charlie blew out exasperatedly - 'They tell us nothing in that office. Treat us like mushrooms, keep us in the dark and feed us shit.'

With that he floored the accelerator propelling the truck forward which sent Jason sprawling in the back.

'Better get your belt on,' Alan advised. Then whispered conspiratorially, 'He drives this thing like it's a giant rally car. If you don't use the seatbelt you will be shaking like a jakey's dug when it's doing a hard shite.'

Belting up, Jason then looked his new workmate over. A bit older than him but not much.
His overalls were wear-worn so he wasn't knew to the job. Not like his duds, brand new and just out the packet. The main thing was he seemed friendly. Some of the old critters he had to deal with at the Recycling Centre were right crabbit old gits. None seemed in the same League of grumpiness as Charlie, or so his reputation decreed.

Once he settled down Jason, was impressed how clean and well fitted the cab was. Big bench seats and separate pouches at the side to store bags and coats. A big contrast to the smelly bit behind them.

Their first stop that morning was in a Council estate. Charlie stamped on the brakes and Jason shot forward, only to be held back by his belt. Alan laughed, he knew what was coming and had braced himself.

Alan urged his new workmate out. 'Right, lets get out. Bins don't empty themselves.'

' Bins? But we are recycling?'

'Recycling today, bins tomorrow. Rubbish, re-cycling, call

it what you want it's all just somebody's waste. My motto though is always the same. At the end of the day, it's all rubbish.'

They jumped out and walked over to the first trolley. The Council had been revolutionary in their approach to Recycling and had won awards for their methods. Instead of individual bins for each type of recycling, they used a trolley with different compartments with separate compartments on the truck for each type.

Alan pulled the trolley to the lorry and started emptying each compartment.

'It's not a spectator sport, Jason. You can join in anytime mate.'

Jason shrugged. 'What do you do?'

'The aim is to put the stuff in the lorry. What, have you never done this before?'

Jason shook his head.

'Have you not been on another run? Where did you come from?'

'I worked up at the Recycling Centre until Friday.'

'The Centre, oh my, that's brain-dead stuff. You will like this better. Okay, it's quite simple. Paper in the top goes in the paper section. See the picture of a newspaper. Plastics and cans in the section with the plastic bottles and cans picture and glass at the bottom in the bit with the big glass bottle.'

'Right. Papers, plastic and cans, bottles.' He pointed them out as he spoke.

'Think I've got it. But what if I get it wrong?'

'Well, you just give the cunts up at the Recycling something to do. Not that I am saying you are a cunt. Or you were a cunt.'

Jason just shrugged. 'What if I find un-recyclables in the recyclables?'

'Good question. Folk will try to dump all sorts of crap in their trolleys. They have their landfill bin but are always trying to get away with shoving other stuff in the trolleys. Right, if you think it's not right, you tell Charlie. He will give you a label that gets stuck on the trolley and we don't empty it. They know why it's not being emptied. Bound to get some down here. These cunts don't give a shit.'

Charlie blasts on the horn.

'Better hurry, lesson over, lets get the trolley's emptied.'

Jason goes to the other side of the road and starts.

Alan is much more experienced and therefore quicker. A few times he has to come across to help Jason catch up. Jason apologised but Alan knew he was getting it.

As the run goes, Jason starts to get a bit quicker. That is until he comes to a trolley that is surrounded by a mass of blue-bottles. Buzzing about, desperate to get at the contents.

Jason knew something wasn't right. 'Alan!' Jason shouted.

Alan hurried over. 'What's wrong? Oh, that doesn't look good,' he said studying the suspect trolley. He carefully opens the top compartment and a swarm of flies shoot out, followed by the smell. 'Oh, fucking shit,' Alan said as he covered his nose and mouth with his hand.

Jason gags and is nearly sick at the stench. 'What is it?'

'Nappy. It's fucking full and not fresh either. Get a label from Charlie.' He flicked the lid back over to contain the smell.

Jason walks round to the lorry door and knocks.

'What's wrong, broke a fingernail. Or have you had enough, want to go home?'

'No, we've got a dirty nappy in the recycling.'

Charlie hands down an orange label and mutters dirty bastards under his breath.

Jason rushed back just as the trolley's owner walks out. She's in her 70's, wearing her old man's tracksuit, hair not combed and smoking a roll up.

'What the fuck's up now? Any excuse and the bins are left. Glass bottle in the plastics or an empty tin in with the glass?'

Alan shook his head. 'There's a dirty nappy.'

The woman starts to lose it. 'Do I look as if I use nappies?'

Jason sighed. 'My gran needs a nappy too. She is inter-continental.'

'Inter-what? You mean incontinent, you fucking half-wit. Well, there is nothing wrong with my bowels.'

'She is senile as well,' he adds, 'doesn't know what she is doing half the time.'

The woman grabs at her head in exasperation. 'So I am incontinent and senile am I. Shitting myself and don't even know I have done it. Fuck me! Where's the boss?'

Alan points to the cab and the woman storms off.

She bangs on the drivers door.

Charlie sticks his head out the window. 'Watch the paintwork!'

'Right, that boy there,' she said, pointing in the direction of the lads.

'Which one?'

'The dopey looking one.'

'Come on Mrs. There are no Einsteins working on the Recycling.'

'The taller one. He is a retard and a cheeky bastard. Said I was incontinent and senile. What are you going to do about it?'

'Firstly, he is not a retard. Maybe he is a bit slow but it's his first day. Secondly, from where I am sitting, he might not be a bad judge of character. So, what am I going to do? Well, I have given the lads a sticker and if there is a soiled nappy in the box we will not be emptying it.'

'You know something, you are a fucking wanker. And a cheeky fucking one at that'

She storms off. When she gets halfway she turns and flashes the bird at Charlie.

Charlie replies with a cheery wave that just gets her angrier.

Back at the trolley, the old crow grabs the nappy, walks over and throws it into her neighbours garden which is unkempt, the lawn uncut and kids outdoor toys are strewn all over. Before it lands it flaps open spreading shite everywhere.

'It will be that trollop's anyway?' she shouts, pointing to the house.

She marches back to the trolley. 'Well, will you empty it now?'

Jason looks in to the paper box. 'No, there is still some jobby juice on the papers.'

'What? Jobby juice. Let me fucking see.' The woman looks in then grabs half of the papers. 'Well?'

Jason takes a look in then grabs the trolley handle. 'That's fine,' then rushes off with it.

When he takes it back emptied the woman grabs it off him and storms away muttering to herself as she goes.

'No Christmas tip from her this year, then,' Alan said.

'What, you get tips from customers just for emptying their recycling?', Jason says excitedly.

'No, I was just pulling your chain. They wouldn't give you a smell of their shit this lot. Sorry, that's all they would give you. Come on, lets get these trolleys emptied.'

As they walk back to the lorry, Alan puts an arm round Jason. 'Might not be as bad at the Recycling centre after all.'

'Oh, no, I like it here. You meet people. At the centre, all you do is deal with rubbish.'

Alan laughs. 'Same here really, just a different kind of rubbish.

They get back to work, emptying the trolleys.

At the end of the road, Alan is ahead of Jason and gets in the cab first.

'Charlie, he is not very strong, is he?'

'Well, you weren't Charles Atlas either when you started.'

'Who is Charles Atlas?'

'Google it. Anyway, the boy is wiry, he will fill out in a couple of months. While we are at the character assassination, I want to give you a bit of advice. Since you started working with me all I ever hear from you is about girls and what you have done to them. Shagged this one, blow job from another. Well, if you ever go near any of my granddaughters I will personally cut off your dick and bollocks and ram them down your throat. Understand?'

'What's brought this on?'

'Well firstly, that boy seems nice and I don't want you corrupting him. Secondly, and more importantly, in the last 6 months all I've heard from you is how you treat woman like bits of meat. You won't do that to any of my kin.'

'I don't know any of your family.'

'Well, for the sake of your health, keep it that way.'

As Jason is getting back in the wagon he hears raised voices. Halfway down the street, the old hag's neighbour has appeared and is shouting.

Charlie turns the lorry around at the end of the street. Just as they drive past the old crones,
her neighbour launches the filled nappy back towards the old hag. The lads could see this ending in blows.

As the Recycling lorry passes Charlie blasts his horn and they all wave out.

The two women pause their hostilities long enough for both to hurl abuse towards the lorry.

Jason and Alan are in stitches laughing. Even Charlie is chuckling.

'That's quality man. Wish I could have recorded it. I hope somebody is getting this on their phone,' Alan said.

Jason looks bemused. 'You mean you can record things like that on your phone.'

'Are you for real? What do you use your phone for?'

'It's only for emergencies. So I can phone or text mum and say if I will be late.'

'No way. That's all you use your phone for, making calls? We are nearly at our break. I will show you what a phone can do at lunchtime.'

Jason jumped in the back of the cab. He was enjoying his first day but now he was ready for something to eat. Before eating, he took out his anti-bacterial gel and cleaned his hands thoroughly.

Alan was staring at him. 'What's that all about?'

'Germs.'

'Fuck off! Did nobody tell you the first thing you have to do is build up an immunity?'

'I'm not going to risk it, I've always used it. Don't want dia-whatsit, you know, the runs.'

'You will grow out of it. Tell him Charlie.'

'That gel stuffs for wee lassies and poofs- which one are you? Not a bumboy I hope.'

'No! No I am not, I am straight,' Jason said, annoyed by the suggestion he was anything else. Upset or not he attacked his sandwiches with gusto. The fresh air had given him a huge appetite.

Alan had perfected the art of eating with one hand and working his phone with the other.

As soon as they had finished eating, Alan beckoned Jase closer and held his phone out so they both could watch.

Jason's eyes widened in disbelief as his new mate showed him Facebook, YouTube and all it's other fancy apps.

'This is a dating app.'

As he scrolled down Jason just managed a 'wow'.

'Are those girls all looking for boyfriends?'

'Well, that is the point of a dating app. Thing is, I've been out with most of them. Got them in my wee black book. Points for how good they were.'

'What kissing, like?'

Alan laughed at his naivety. 'No, the ones I've pumped, had sex with.'

'All of those?'

'No, not them all but most of the good looking ones. Didn't have sex with them all, some were only good enough for a blow job. Saving themselves for their Wedding Day and all that shit.'

Alan then produced a dog-eared little black book from his backpack.

'Are you sure they just don't fancy you and that's why they don't want to do it with you?'

'Don't fancy me! Come on, look at me. What's not to fancy?'

Charlie, without looking up from his phone, said 'Want a list?'

'Could you get me on one of those sites, Alan?'

'Of course, man. Right, let me see your phone.'

Jason searched his backpack and pulled out a small, black phone in a leather case. He hands it to Alan.

'Holy shit. This is a museum piece. Where the fuck did you get this antique?'

'It was my mum's old one.'

Alan lifts it up. 'Charlie, look at this.'

The driver looks up from his own phone. 'Is it wind up one?', he said after glancing up, before going back to his own phone.

'Right, chum. You will need to get a real phone before you can go on-line. How much is your contract for this-fifty pence a month?'

'No, it's pay as you go.'

'Pay as you go? Pay as you fucking go. No way man. I didn't think anyone was still on pay as you go.' Alan looks at his own phone, puzzled. 'Oh, hold on until I check the calendar- no it is the 2019. I thought for a minute we had all been transported back about 20 years. Pay as you go?'

'So, what kind is yours?'

'It's an iphone but it doesn't matter what kind you get, as long as you get access to the Internet so you can get Facebook and all that stuff. Make sure it can do all that.'

'Right, I'll get one after work.'

Next morning Jason was all excited. When he arrived he got in the cab desperate to show his new phone. However, before he could even get it out, Alan signalled something was up. Jason was hardly seated when the bin lorry shot forward.

Alan whispered, 'Charlie is in one of his moods. Think he's having a bit of marital strife.

You can show me your phone at lunch. Just don't rile the big man.'

The first time they stopped at traffic lights, Jason leaned forward. 'Is everything okay Charlie.'

Alan held his head in his hands. What was his new mate doing, talk about pouring petrol on a fire to put it out.

'You don't have a woman in your life so you wouldn't understand.'

'I've got my mother. I live with her.'

'Not the same, son. Unless you are riding her. Or at least trying too.'

'No, but I am a good listener, so if you want to talk about it, you know I'm here for you.'

Charlie shook his head and drove off when the lights changed. Alan couldn't believe his new mates naivety.

Charlie had mellowed by lunchtime. The atmosphere in the cab had changed and as soon as food was finished, Jason got his new phone out.

'Wow, now this is a phone. How much is this costing you a month?'

'Fifty pounds.'

'Fifty quid a month? How can you afford that? You live with your mum, right?'

Jason nodded.

'How much do you give her for your keep?'

'A hundred.'

'A hundred a week?'

'No, a month.'

'A month? A month. Is she looking for a lodger?'

'No. Why are you looking for somewhere?'

'At that price- yes. My mother takes £300 a month and I still have to buy my own products.'

'Products?'

'Hair gel, deodorants, after shave, cologne, all that stuff.'

'Mum just gets me Mum.'

Alan despaired of his new mate. 'Anyway, give me your phone and lets get you set up.'

Jason hands over the new handset.

Alan was getting exasperated with Jason 'You have to unlock it first,' he said, giving him it back.

Jason takes a bit of paper from his backpack and slowly puts the number in then hands it back.

Alan, being a whiz quickly sets up the Apps Jason will need. 'Right, Dating site. What kind of site do you want?'

'What do you mean?'

'There are dating sites for whatever your fancy is. Romance, woman after sex, men after sex, married women wanting affairs, cougars after young bucks. So, do you want love and romance or wham, bang, thank you ma'am.'

Jason was quiet as he tried to take in what had been on the list Alan had read.

'So what is it? Love and Romance or is it just your hole you want? '

'And they say romance is dead,' Charlie said, without even looking up from his own phone.

'I just want to meet a nice girl and settle down.'

'Don't recommend it myself. Jason, my friend, you are like me, a young buck. We should be out sowing our wild oats, every chance we can get. Every hole is a goal, that's my motto.'

'I'm not into all that sleeping around stuff. Women are not sex objects.'

They were interrupted by Charlie giving him a round of applause. 'Well said, young man.'

Alan just shrugged. 'Still, if it's love you want, it's best you sign up with Kissing Frogs.

'Kissing Frogs, what's that all about?'

'Kissing Frogs, surely you have heard the saying, you have to kiss a lot of frogs to find a prince. Or in your case a princess. At least I assume it's a princess you are after.'

'Yes, it's a young lady I am after. I'm certainly not gay. It's a woman I am after. But do I really need to kiss a frog?'

'No, it's just the name of the site. Right, lets go. Full name?'

'Jason Dux. D-u-x.'

'Really? Is that your name, Dux. Have you got a middle name?'

'Cox. C-o-x.'

'Jason Cox Dux. I think it's best we skip the middle name.'

'Why' Jason asked.

Alan tried not to laugh. 'Just trust me on that one. Next, date of birth?'

Jason closed his eyes and thought about it. 'Sixth of November,1997.'

'You are 3 months younger than me!'

'No way. I thought I was way younger than you, a couple of years at least.'

'That's my adult aura,' Alan said proudly.

Charlie chipped in with another one of his remarks- 'Did you say horror.'

'Thinks he is a comedian,' Alan whispered. 'Right, this App you just have to answer 10 questions and they will match you up with your ideal woman. Now, favourite food?'

'A fish supper.'

'No, you can't say that. You know, eating at the chippy. Are you going to take a bird to Aldo's chippy. Table for two, two fish suppers and a bottle of Vimto.'

Jason just stares at Alan uncomprehending.

'Where would you normally take a girl? Nando's, Chinese, Indian?'

'I've never taken a girl out.'

'You mean for a meal.'

'No, never taken a girl out.' He waited for laughter. Jason looked surprised. 'I thought you would have laughed. You know, saddo, twenty two years old and never been kissed.'

Alan looked up at Charlie via the drivers mirror. They were making a mental note of storing this nugget to be mentioned at the most embarrassing moment.

'Listen, don't worry, we will soon sort that out. Won't we

Charlie.'

Charlie just grunted.

'Back to business. Imagine you hit her, you give her the chat. She agrees to a date, where do you take her?'

'Chinese. Can I choose Chinese?'

'You, son, can take her wherever you want. Right, Chinese it is. Next, favourite drink?'

'Buckfast.'

Alan shakes his head again. 'Oh, fuck. Right, you might not agree but Buckfast says ned to me. Is that what you are looking for- a neddette?'

'No, I am not a ned, I just like the taste.'

'I am not saying you are a ned but society would. So, if you are not a ned and you are on a date, in the Chinese restaurant, the waiter comes over. Madam. White wine. Certainly, and for you, Sir? Buckfast. Certainly Sir, just wait until I nip down to the local Spar and get a bottle.'

'Maybe you are right.'

'So, what I would suggest is red wine. After all, Buckie is a type of wine, isn't it?'

'Suppose so.'

'Right, now, favourite film?'

'Trainspotting. The first one, though, the second one is crap.'

Alan shook his head again. 'Right, although they want to know your favourite film, you have to think about your target audience, that is the girl. What kind of girl would watch Trainspotting?'

'I don't know. Somebody that likes Scottish films.'

'Oh, right, a nice wee Scottish film about druggies. No, you need to think of a soppy one. One that says this guy is romantic. Likes a happy ending. What about Dirty Dancing?'

'Never seen it.'

'Ghost?'

'No. Is that not a horror?'

'No, it's a Romance. Woman want love and romance. If

you say that's what you want then you need to give them it. Now, have you never watched a romantic film?'

Jason suddenly has a rush of inspiration. 'Baywatch!'

'Baywatch romantic? All right, that's close enough. The thing is if you want to appeal to a woman you have to think a bit like a woman.'

'Think like a woman, right I will do that.'

'Next, an easy one. Favourite colour.'

'Pink.'

'Pink is your favourite colour? Are you sure you are not gay?'

'You just said think like a woman! Women like pink. Make your mind up.'

'No, you need to think what a woman wants in a man not what she likes for herself. She wants a strong man, who will protect and provide for her. Think of a manly colour.'

'What colours are manly? What about blue then.'

'Blue is as manly as fuck. We have blue overalls because we are manly men.'

Charlie looks round and sniggers. 'You two are so manly. Fuck me, I've shit harder things.'

Alan can't resist answering back. 'How is it I get so many birds, then?'

'Obviously it's because they are desperate. Or have no taste. Or are desperate and have no taste.'

Jason just shrugs, no way was he arguing with Charlie.

'Right, Jason, next, film star.'

'Vin Diesel.'

'Well, I suppose some women go for that type. He might be bald but he definitely is not gay. Next, TV show.'

'Only Fools.'

'I suppose you can't go wrong with a bit of Del-boy. Right, singer and song.'

'Meat Loaf and Bat out of Hell.'

'God, that's a tune.'

'Yeah, my dad used to sing it all the time.'

Charlie made one of his rare utterances. 'You know there is some hope.'

Both lads were stunned by this. They looked at each other but neither knew what he was getting at. Alan spoke, 'What do you mean?'

'Well, it's a classic piece of Rock and Roll and you both appreciate it. I'm just surprised, that's all.'

'What, our taste in everything else is, what, shit?'

'Well, Alan, you said it.'

'Right, Jason, back to the job in hand. Favourite season?'

'Eh, that's got to be pepper.'

'No, season of the year. Spring, Summer, Autumn, Winter.'

'Right, summer. That would be funny, sprinkle a little summer on my soup.'

'Okay, but don't try stand up. Lastly, occupation.'

'Bin man?'

'Right, here's where you jazz it up a bit. Binman is what you are but it's no, well sexy.'

'Sexy?'

'Okay, maybe not sexy because no matter how you dress up, what we do, emptying bins, will never be sexy. What you want is a bit more kudos. Sounds better than it is. You see when I fill in forms I say I am a Recycling Administrator.'

'Oh, that's good. Can I be a Recycling Administrator too.'

'Of course. Right, that's you done.'

'So, what happens next?'

'Well, your details are all in. It's been sent. You just need to wait until all the sexy ladies start lining up for a bit of the old Jason boy. It says your profile will be loaded within the next two days then we can get started.'

Jason took his phone back and put it in his backpack. 'I can't wait,' he said excitedly.

Charlie turned to them. 'Right, if you two are quite finished, get out there and administer some recycling into the truck.'

Next morning, Charlie and Alan are in the bin lorry waiting, Jason nearly pulls the door off its hinges, in his rush to get in.

'Alan, Alan, there are girls in my App. What do I do? What do I do?'

'Right, chill. Take a deep breath.'

Charlie started the lorry up and it shot forward.

Jason was again propelled across the back seat and after bouncing back, landed on the floor in a heap.

'For fucks sake, Charlie,' Jason shouted.

The big man just grinned. 'Here is a concept for you. Turn up on time. Or if you want to fanny about on your phone, come early.'

Alan helped Jason up. 'We will sort it at lunch,' he reassured him.

Once again their travels took them to a run down part of town. Jason stared out of the side window without saying anything.

Alan, reading his mind, decided a bit of a wind-up was on the cards. 'Rough here. Sometimes the trolleys are up on bricks.'

'Really?'

'Oh aye. If you see a dog with three legs and one eye, chances are it will be called Lucky.'

'Do you think there will be any strange stuff today?'

'Jason, my son, there is always strange stuff, only the degree of strangeness varies. One day up here we thought we saw a kangaroo.'

'A kangaroo here?'

'No, turned out it was a greyhound doing a shit. But they look the same.'

Jason didn't get the joke and got out of the wagon very warily, looking around as he did so.

However, the morning seemed to be going quite normally

until Jason found a strange object propped up against one of the trolleys.

He shouted Alan, who was on the opposite side of the road.

'What is it?'

Jason shrugged. 'I don't know, that's why I shouted you. Looks like a leg.'

Alan rushed over and picked it up. 'Ho, ho, it's an artificial leg.'

'Do we put it in the Recycling?'

'What? No, this could be worth something. Tell you what, we will put it in the plastics and sneak it into the back of the cab at lunch.'

'Where will we sell it, a second hand shop?'

'Here, that's a good one. Unless we find a second leg shop. Anyway, we could sell it as a Christmas gift for somebody. Not the main gift, just a stocking filler.'

Alan laughed at his own joke but Jason didn't see the funny side. They put the leg in the back of the lorry and carried on.

The lorry turned at the end of the street and headed back out of the scheme.

At the point where they had found the artificial leg, there was a one legged man in the middle of the road, balancing with one arm over a crutch, the other waving desperately. As the lorry got nearer he started waving both arms.

Charlie stopped the lorry just as the man succumbed to the forces of gravity and landed on his side, on top of his crutch that landed before him. He rolled onto his side then struggled to get back upright.

With the lorry parked, all three scrambled out of the lorry and ran round to help the stricken amputee.

Charlie lifted the man as if he was a featherweight although he was carrying a bit of timber.

'What's up old man? Feeling suicidal?', Charlie asked.

'No, my leg.'

'What about it? Seemed okay until you started waving about like a demented scarecrow in a whirlwind.'

'No, my other leg! The artificial one. The wife said she put it out for the Recycling.'

'Why?'

'She found out I was knobbing Kathy next door.'

The man turned to face his house and the three workers followed his gaze. At the window was a sour faced woman, arms crossed and not very happy looking.

Their eyes then went next door an older lady looked out, smiling and gave a little wave.

Jason spoke and said what the others were thinking. 'Is she not a lot older than you.'

The disabled man then spouted his logic. 'They are the best ones to knob. The old one's don't yell, they don't tell and they are as grateful as Hell. And as Kathy is going a bit senile, so she doesn't remember too well.'

'So, where's the leg?' Charlie asked.

Jason ran to the back and retrieved it.

'We were keeping it for safe keeping,' Alan lied.

The grateful guy then lay on the road and took off his trousers. While he was down to his pants the two young one's stared at the huge bulge hidden by a thin layer of boxer shorts.

Leg strapped on, Charlie helped him up again. As he stood up, eyes turned to his neighbour Kathy, who now stood at her living room window. She had dis-robed and stood naked. She cupped her drooping tits then beckoned her neighbour back for more sex.

Jason was mesmerised. This was the first naked body he had ever clapped eyes on. Sure he had seen plenty nude books and sex on films but this was real, in the flesh. He was amazed at the porcelain whiteness of the skin and the mahogany darkness of her nipples that hung at the end of her saggy tits.

The spell was broken by the one legged man's wife who had left the house and was yelling in at Kathy, who reached over and pulled her curtains shut. 'Right, Romeo, in there,' she said pointing to their house.

Romeo limped off, muttering he would need to give her a good pumping to shut her up.

Charlie and the lads went back into the cab. As he started the engine, he announced they were due a break after the trauma.

Alan spoke first. 'Did you see that old Kathy's droopy tits. That old cow must be over 70. Can you imagine still doing it at that age?'

Jason realised he had a bit of a stiffy. Luckily for him the bagginess of his new overalls hid his embarrassment. Sure, he knew Alan had been good with him, not slagging him over his virginity but if he knew that old Kathy's body gave him a hard-on, boy would he rip the pish. He whispered to Alan, 'Do you think Charlie is still, you know, doing it?'

Alan whispered back. 'Yes, but not as often as he wants. That's why he is always in a mood.'

Just at that, Charlie parked the lorry up. He turned to the lads. ' What about old Kathy? That image will live with me for ever. My God, her tits were like Spaniels ears and her bush, that was like one of they Al-Qa'ida. Big, grey, hairy bush. Need a cuppa to get over it.'

Jason remembered his new phone. 'Alan, Alan, can we look at these girls now.'

'Sure, get your phone out.'

Jason's hands shook now with excitement. He managed to unlock it and open the Dating App page. Alan took the phone off him and flicked through the pictures of the girls. He then got his small black book out of his backpack and checked it against the pictures. As he moved through them he would say- yes, yes as he did so.

'Do you know a lot of them?'

'Know them? I have pumped most of them, well the ones that were good enough.' He indicated his wee black book. 'That's what this book is, a record of every woman I have pumped and how I rated them. From age 17 to 43.'

'You have honestly had sex with a woman of 43. My God, my mother is 43.'

'Oh, what's her name? Better check.'

'You better be joking.' Jason was clenching his fists now, ready to pounce. Nobody dissed him mum.

'Relax. It was a one off when I was on holiday in Benidorm.'

'Well, it's still gross. Bet you sneak back for a poke at Kathy.'

'Ha fucking ha. My motto is every hole is a goal but that is an exception.'

'Bet you sneak back,' Charlie said, then laughed at his own joke.

'Right, so what do I do with this App?' Jason said, keen to get started.

'Okay, so if you see a girl you really like then you swipe the bit at the bottom. If she likes you, she swipes too and you will get a notification with either her phone number or email address. You start texting or emailing then if you agree, you meet up. Or you don't. Up to you.'

'Can I not just swipe them all and see who replies?'

'Oh, no. I'm a player but even I wouldn't try that stunt. One at a time. Now the first girl, your top match, Carly.'

'I like her.'

'Sure but look here, favourite food, Krispy Kreme Donuts. She must be a right chunker.'

'Chunker?'

'You know, big girl. And guaranteed chunkers just get chunkier. Whose next?'

'But I like the look of Carly.'

'Look mate, I wouldn't be your mate if I let you get landed with a big fat chunker.'

'Right, then, next is Elaine.'

'Blond, buck teeth?'

'Yes.'

'Spunk bucket. If it's a guaranteed shag you want, swipe

her.'

'No, that's not what I'm after, I told you that.'

'Well she is not the type to settle down. Next then.'

'Eva.'

'Red hair, glasses.'

'That's her.'

'Frigid. Won't let you anywhere near her fud. What she will do is wank you off then when you come, she will lick it off your belly.'

'That's gross. Is that true? How do you know?'

'I was out with her twice. But I was red raw after it. Thought she was going to pull the bloody thing off.'

'Right, Wendy is next.'

'Wendy? Wendy? I don't know a Wendy. Let me see. Right fit, she is. Certainly don't know her or I would have defo pumped her if I got the chance. Tell you what, if you don't go for her, I will.'

'Right, that's her swiped. So, how long before she will get back to me?'

'Well, if she gets back to you, she might not. She has to like the look of you as well remember. Anyway, don't you worry, she will get back to you, I have a good feeling.'

Jason was waiting at the bin lorry even before Charlie got there the next morning.

Charlie looked him up and down. 'What's up with you, pish the bed?'

'No, I couldn't wait to tell Alan the news. I've got a date for tonight.'

'Good, but watch Alan. Between you and me, he is only out for himself. I would just watch yourself.'

Just at that, Alan made an appearance.

'Alan, Alan, I've got a date for tonight.'

'Wendy is it?'

'Yes. We are going to the Oak Tavern. Just for a drink.'

'Oh, just for a drink. Right. Just remember to take condoms.'

'No, it's only a drink.'

'Look, it's the oldest story. Boy meets girl, girl falls for boy, boy likes girl. Back to hers, kiss kiss, bang bang. Thing is you must have protection. '

'You think so? I don't really approve of sex on the first date anyway.'

'Right, but you have been texting.'

'Yes.'

'Well, in modern parlance, that's the equivalent of a date, so, technically tonight will be your second date.'

'Really? Texting is like a first date. I didn't know that. Anyway, I still don't think it's right to just jump into bed with somebody, you know, if you don't love them.'

'Maybe that's why you are a virgin, my son.'

Jason was raging. Right at that minute he wanted to punch his mate. Sure he had been quiet when he opened up about his virginity but all the time must Alan had been waiting his chance to poke fun at him. He thought hard before he said anything, it had to be good.

'I would rather be a virgin than the male equivalent of a slut,' Jason said.

Alan's mouth fell open. It only closed when Charlie started clapping.

'Bravo. He needed telling.'

Things between the two lads were frosty all morning after that but after lunch they went back to normal. Alan was ribbing him gently about his date and popping his cherry. Jason remained insistent it wouldn't be happening.

At the end of the run, Jason was desperate to get away. As he reached for the door, Alan pulled him back. 'Good luck tonight and don't forget your condoms,' Alan said.

'Don't have any and I won't need them anyway.'

'Here,' Alan handed him a pack of three. 'Please, take

them. If you get carried away, better to be safe than get a dose.'

'A dose?'

'An STD.'

Jason gave another of his now famous blank looks.

'A sexually transmitted disease.'

'All right, I will take then but I won't need them.'

Jason left and Alan laughed.

'What the fuck are you up to?' Charlie asked.

'Charlie, I am just helping the boy on the path to divine pumping.'

'You know this girl he is going out with then.'

'Oh yes, at school we called her Wendy one tit.'

'She only had one tit?'

'No. All the lads at school went out with her, she was, how would you say, popular as in school bike, you know, everybody was riding her. Well, not everybody. The thing was when you kissed her you squeezed a tit. If you picked the correct one she let you shag her, pick the wrong one and you didn't.'

'Did you pick the correct one?'

'I'm not a gambler. I grabbed both. Popped my cherry with her. A knee trembler round the back of the Scout hall.'

'Do you think Jason will be safe with her?'

'Well, she has two kids now so she has probably settled down.'

'Tell you what, if anything bad happens to Jason, you will have to answer to me. I kind of like that boy.'

'Listen, the worst that will happen is that he won't be Jason the virgin boy any more.'

Jason paced up and down outside the Oak Tavern. For more than ten minutes he'd stepped back and forth. She wasn't going to turn up, he knew it. The longer he went on, the more he was convinced she wasn't coming. He was so engrossed in this that he never noticed a woman watching.

'Jason?'

'Oh, Wendy?'

As he walked over he saw she was pretty. Prettier than she had looked in the pic on his phone. She was about the same age as him and sexily dressed. She had a black dress, white top that barely held her ample breasts. His eyes stared at them just a bit too long. When she smiled big dimples appeared on her cheeks.

'I like your dimples,' he said by way of a compliment.

'I've never heard them called that before,' she said looking down at her chest.

Jason felt his face redden. This was all so new to him. 'No, not your eh things, I meant the dimples on your pretty face. When you smile, you have lovely dimples.'

'Charmer.'

Not sure what do do next, Jason reached out a hand to shake. Wendy had other ideas and grabbed his face and turned it, planting a smacker on his lips.

'Start as we mean to go on,' she said winking.

Jason had been worried about Wendy not turning up. As they walked into the pub he realised he was even more nervous now that she had turned up.

'Drink,' he said.

'That's why we go to pubs. Gin and tonic. Best make it a double.'

Jason walked to the bar as Wendy got them a table. After ordering her drink, Jason wondered what would be best for himself. He settled on a bottle of lager, didn't want to be running to the pisser all night. As he lifted it from the bar he realised his hand was shaking.

Wendy meantime had made herself at home. Her jacket was over the back of her chair and she was settled back. Jason sat her drink down and sat opposite.

'What no straw or umbrella?'

'Oh, sorry, I will get them.' He was halfway out of his seat before Wendy grabbed his sleeve.

'Sit down. I'm only pulling your plonker.'

'Oh, right.'

'With a bit of luck it will be your other plonker I will be pulling later.'

Jason flushed again. He didn't usually embarrass easily but Wendy was making an easy job of it.

'So, what do you do?' he asked. He couldn't think of anything else to ask. Why did he not ask Alan for some tips. Mind you, he thought, his first line would have been what's your favourite sexual position.

Wendy took a large gulp of drink. 'God, I needed that. Well, right now, I am between jobs. I was training to be a nail technician before I got pregnant the first time. I'm too old to go back to that.'

'No, you are still young. I just started a new job recently.'

'Oh, what do you do?'

'I am an eh., Recycling Administrator.'

'What does that mean?'

'Well, I get Recycling and Administer it into the correct types.'

'Sounds a bit like a kind of binman.'

'Well, I am a kind of binman. In fact I am a bin man.'

'Why not say so? Bin man's a good job. Good pay working for the council and a pension at the end of it.'

'Yes, you're right, it is a good job.'

Jason was feeling a bit less nervous now and took a sip of beer. That was when he realised Wendy's glass was nearly empty.

'Another drink?'

'Oh yes. That hit the spot. It's good to relax without the kids.'

'Kids? How many do you have?'

'Two. At the moment. They are both away at their dads for the weekend so I have the house to myself.' She winked and smiled.

Jason was still determined not to go back with her but realised now was not the time to tell her. He went to the bar and returned with another G and T, this time with a straw and umbrella.

'Oh, that's nice. You are really nice.'

Jason was well chuffed, he'd never been called nice by a girl before. Mind you, he had never really been called anything by a girl before.

The young couple got on like a house on fire. Jason thought it would be hard talking to a girl
but Wendy seemed more like one of his mates. Everybody said women didn't understand guys but she seemed too.

Wendy checked her phone then drained her glass. She had finished off 5 doubles while Jason
just managed 4 bottles.

'My taxi is coming in 5 minutes, are you coming out with me.'

'Oh, right.' Jason didn't know that was how dates ended. The woman driving off into the moonlight waving from the back of a taxi while the man waved back pondering if this is the last he will see her or if there was enough spark to kindle something more.

Outside it was a bit chilly. Wendy led Jason into the nearby bus shelter. She moved in close and kissed him. Their kissing continues. For all his intentions otherwise, he started to get aroused.

'Now, Jason, you might think me forward but I want you to come back to my place with me.'

Jason went to say something but Wendy kissed him again. She was a good kisser and although Jason was debuting on the kissing front he was learning fast.

'If not, I hope you will at least share a taxi because I don't have the fare.'

'I would like to come back with you.'

Jason couldn't believe what he had just said. Especially as he knew what would inevitably happen, whether he wanted to or not. The moment for him was spoiled by the taxi drawing up right behind them and the driver leaning on the horn. The blast had both of them nearly jumping out of their skins.

'You are a fucking prick, Andy,' Wendy shouted in to the laughing cabbie.

The journey was quicker than Jason wanted it to be. The nerves were starting to build. His hand, that rested in Wendy's, started to sweat.

When the cab stopped, Jason reached into his wallet for the cash to pay for the fare. As he did so the condoms he put their for safe keeping fell out. In his scrambled mind he wondered if this was a sign. Tell the driver to drive on, take him home.

'Oh, looks like it's your lucky night tonight,' Andy said, winking conspiratorially.   Jason didn't know the protocol regarding tipping drivers but Andy had lost any chance he had of a tip. Jason gave him the correct money and scooped the condoms up. He put them in his trouser pocket so they would be handier.

Wendy stood at the front door waiting for him. She told him to use the downstairs toilet.

He pushed as much urine out as he could. After shaking, he thought he better dry it so used the towel over the radiator. Then he put a bit of toothpaste on his finger and scrubbed his teeth. After gargling he wiped his mouth on the towel before realising it was the bit he used to dry his willie.

Wendy was waiting outside the toilet door. She ordered him to go up to the bedroom, strip off and get into bed while she used the lavvy.

Jason walked slowly up the stairs. Tonight was going to be thee night. The night he lost his virginity. His heart was thumping so hard he could feel the pulse in his ears.

The bedroom was neat and tidy. It was dimly lit by a lamp on Wendy's bedside table. Jason stripped and put his clothes on a neat pile at the bottom of the bed. One of the condoms was retrieved from his pocket and slipped below his pillow for easy access.

He heard the bathroom door close and Wendy approaching up the stairs that creaked as she stood on them signalling her impending arrival.

She walked in wearing only a black bra and pants. Frilly, sexy stuff but Jason was putting all his attention on what was in it. Her skin so white in contrast to what little material covered her sexy bits. He was hardening by the second. He gave a silent prayer to his stiffening cock that it didn't let him down and he didn't come too early.

Stopping at the bottom of the bed, Wendy reached behind and unclipped her bra. It fell from her arms to the floor, exposing two well proportioned breasts. She rubbed them as they were tense after being cooped up in the tight bra all night. Next her hands slid down her body and slipped her pants over her hips and then let them fall to the floor to join the discarded bra.

Jason stared in awe of her body. She wasn't fat, save for a bit of a baby belly. His attention was drawn to the sex between her legs. She was bald down there. Shaved clean.

Wendy walked along the opposite side of the bed and pulled back the covers that were covering his modesty.

'What are you doing with those on?' She gestured to the big white y-fronts he still had on.

'Are you going to poke 'it' out of the wee hole in the middle?' she asked, laughing as she said so.

Jason embarrassedly slipped them off, struggling to get them past his stiff member and dropped them at the side of the bed.

Wendy slipped onto the bed and joined them. She kissed him and slid her hand down and cupped his balls.

'My, my, these need emptied.' Her hand then moved up and grabbed the shaft that was gaining in girth by the second. 'Think you are ready,' she said. 'Don't want you spurting before you get it in. Have you got a condom?'

Jason reached below the pillow and retrieved the foil pouch.

'Watch this.' With that Wendy took the rubber off him. She opened the pack with her teeth then threw it away. She put the condom in her mouth then proceeded to put it on Jason's erect penis.

Rolling on her back, she instructed Jason to put it in.

Jason took up position between her legs and moved up until he was ready to get started. He pushed it in and thought he was doing well until Wendy stopped him.

'That's my bum!' She said then reached down and put it at the right entrance and guided it home.

Now he was in, Jason started very energetically.

'Wow, slow down. You will be finished in a jiffy.'

Jason slowed and smiled. This was it, the moment he'd dreamed off since puberty. Sex. He was having sex. Quite quickly though he forgot the warning and his thrusting got faster and faster then bang, he was finished. It was only a few minutes but it was magic. He had finally done it, he was no longer a virgin. Pulling out, he rolled over on his back, pretty proud of himself.

'Are you quite happy with that?' Jason asked.

'Well, you forgot something very important.'

'What?'

'Me! Sex is an act between two, we are both supposed to enjoy it.'

'Did you not enjoy it?'

'Oh, I was just starting to get going when you finished.'

'Sorry.'

'It's okay. Right, go down to the toilet, get rid of that johnny, freshen up and come back up and we will start Lesson 2.'

Jason set off down the stairs, holding the rubber in place as it threatened to slip from the now flaccid penis. In the toilet, he rolled the condom off and dropped it down the toilet. As it flushed, he washed his cock in the sink. Before going back up the stairs, he checked down the toilet pan. The pink balloon was still there. Now, however it was 5 times the size, full now with a mixture of sperm and water.

Realising he couldn't leave it there, he lifted it out of the water and drained it. He then wrapped it in toilet paper then flushed again. This time it disappeared. 'Result, he said, congratulating himself.

Walking back up the stairs he realised how good sex was. No wonder Alan was chasing it all the time. The feelings he had when Wendy touched him had been amazing.

Wendy lay in bed, still naked, waiting on his return.

Jason lay beside her.

'Your first time, wasn't it.'

Jason nodded, suddenly feeling a bit embarrassed.

'You did okay. No, in fact you did more than okay. So, is this also your first time on a Dating App?'

'Yes. My workmate Alan Baker helped me get on it.'

'Alan Barker from Gatesbury?'

'Yes. Do you know him?'

'God, yes. I popped his cherry at school. It was after the Third Year disco. He wasn't as good as you. Or as big. In fact we called him Stinky Pinky because it was so wee.'

'Funny, he told me he never knew you.'

'Too embarrassed after his flop. He was the same with all the other girls. In, out, shake it all about. Hopeless. That's why he never dates them more than once, it's the girls that don't want to see him again.'

'He makes out he is a real stud.'

'A lot of men talk a good game. I prefer one who plays a good game like you. Now, lets see if you are ready to go again.'

Jason sat on the bottom of the steps in Wendy's hall putting on his shoes. Wendy had added a dressing gown to her bra and pants. She leaned forward and kissed him on the brow.

'Jason, I hope you take this the right way and don't think you are any kind of failure but I don't think we should see each other again. There is somebody out there for you but it's not me. I hope tonight helped you and you can find the right woman for you.'

Jason stood up and took her in his arms. He kissed her and simply said 'Thanks, I hope you find the right man.'

'Well, it's not for the want of trying. Good luck.'

As Jason walked up the path, he felt 10 foot tall. He left home that night a boy but was returning a man. Wendy had offered to get him a taxi but he insisted on walking home. That was fine for the first mile but the 6 miles in front of him suddenly seemed to be a long trek. Made worse when the rain joined the swirling wind. It still didn't put the smile off his face.

Monday morning and Jason was at the depot before Alan. Charlie was outside talking to one of the other drivers when Alan climbed into the cab.

'You look like the cat that got the cream. Did you score on Friday?' Alan asked.

Jason decided not to divulge what Wendy had said about him, good to keep something up his up sleeve. His lose of virginity was not for discussion either.

'No, she was a lovely girl but not the girl for me. No, the reason I am smiling is because I contacted Carly. We have been chatting all weekend and are going out for a drink on Friday.'

'This Carly one, is she the one I thought was a chunker?'

'Yes but only you think she is a chunker. I think she is what she is. Beauty is skin deep. '

'Did you ask her, you know, if she was a chunker?'

'No!'

'All right, calm down, I was just pulling your chain.'

'She said Friday but I wanted to go out before then.'

'Wow, just cool your jets. Friday seems okay.'

'You are right, play the cool guy.'

'So, Friday night, what's the plan?'

'She is from Kilbride. She is suggesting the new cocktail bar.'

'Cocktail bar. That means money. She isn't going to be a cheap date. Right, I will spend all week schooling you in the art of dating.'

'No. No thanks. I am going to be my own man.'

'Good luck with that. Well, at least you can't blame me when it all fucks up.'

Wednesday morning and Jason is late. Charlie and Alan are in the cab and the driver is not happy.

As he gets in he apologises.'Sorry Charlie, I couldn't sleep last night.'

'Couldn't sleep doesn't empty bins.' With that Charlie drove the lorry off, throwing Jason backwards again.

'What's his beef,' Jason whispered to Al.

'Phones been going off all morning. I think he has fallen out with his old Dutch. Anyway, what were you up to last night, you look like death warmed up? Chugging the chicken or phone sex with Carly?'

'No, we were just texting. Anyway, I don't know how to sext.'

'Want me to show you?'

'No, she is not like that. And neither am I.'

'They are all like that once you get them started.'

Next morning at the Recycling Depot, Jason is pacing back and forth, waiting for Alan to arrive.

'What's wrong, is somebody dead?'

'No, no, I wanted to ask you something before we get to work.'

'Right, private like. Do you want to learn how to sext?'

'No. Listen, what are you doing tomorrow night?'

'Need to check my calendar, why?'

'Well, Carly has suggested we make our date a foursome and she asked if I had an older mate to buddy up with her best friend.'

'Buddy up?'

'That's what she called it.'

'So, who is she, the best friend?'

'She hasn't said, just that it's her best pal. So, if it's her best pal she must be nice.'

'She better not be a chunker. I am warning you. If I agree to go and she is some kind of minger I will be out of there like a whippet.'

'Her friend will be nice. Right, I will buy the first 2 rounds.'

'Okay, I will buddy up, as you say, but you are buying the first 3 rounds.'

'Agreed!'

Friday night and the lads are standing at the bar in the cocktail lounge. They are drinking pints of lager.

'Jason my boy, we can't drink pints when the girls turn up. We will have to go on to cocktails next.'

'What are cocktails like?'

'They are just fruit juice really, with of course a bit of booze in it. Start with a Strawberry Daquiari. It just tastes like strawberrys. You do like strawberrys?'

'Don't mind them. Is that it, they are just like strawberrys.'

'Well, with a little kick.'

The door of the Bar opens and a pleasant looking, slightly plump girl turns up. Jason recognises her from her dating app picture. He gets off the stool to welcome her.

Alan pulls him over and whispers to him, 'She is a bit of a chunker. Her mate better not be one or I am out of here.'

Jason and Carly come together rather embarrassedly as they try the air kissing thing.

'Carly, this is my friend Alan.'

They simply nod to each other and mouth hello.

'Mums just paying the taxi.'

'Your mum! I thought it was your best friend.'

'My mum is my best friend.'

Alan is horrified. Behind Carly's back he mouths to Jason - am out of here. He then drains his pint, ready to make his escape.

The pub door opens and a gorgeous, blond 40 something lady breezes into the bar. She has a gorgeous figure and carries it with the air of somebody who knows how to use it to her advantage. She walks seductively, hips swaying and every head in the place turns. All the guys wishing they were with her, the women wishing they were her.

'There is mum now,' Carly said proudly.

'Your mum. Wow!' Alan said then stood with his mouth hanging open.

Carly introduced them. 'Mum, this is Jason and his friend, Alan.'

'Carly, dear, when we are out, it's not mum, it's Angela.'

'Sorry mum, I forgot.'

Alan managed to pull himself out of his stupor. 'Angela, that's a lovely name.'

Angie shrugged. 'Where are the cocktails, my mouth is like an Arab's sandal.'

Jason and Carly look at each other, quite embarrassed while Alan laughs as if it's the funniest thing he had ever heard.

'Right,' Alan said, 'What are we all drinking? I will get these.'

'I fancy sex on the beach,' Angela said.

Alan laughed embarrassingly loudly before ordering the cocktails.

'Thought you wanted a drink first.'

Alan and Angela laughed embarrassingly loudly while Jason and Carly cringed.

They settle down at a table, Jason and Carly sitting close together and Alan and Angela on the opposite side of the booth.

'So, what is it you do, Angela?' Alan asked.

'Alan, we are not here to talk business but seeing you ask I am the HR manager for a large engineering firm. What about yourself?'

'Oh Jason and I are in the Recycling business.'

'Oh right, I thought you had got that jacket out of a skip. Or was it a charity shop.'

Alan was horrified and looked down at his jacket to find out what was wrong with it.

'This cost me 50 quid,' Alan said in defence of his jacket that he thought was on trend.

'Mum, stop winding Alan up. She's terrible, isn't she, Jason.'

'No, I think she is quite funny. It does look as if it's come out of a skip. No your mum is funny. Not like my mum. My mum is quite boring.'

'Sometimes I wish she was boring. She wasn't like this until dad left.'

'He left her. What for? Another woman?'

'Yes. His secretary.'

'I would never leave you.' Jason started blushing. 'I mean if we were, you know, married.'

'No, I don't think you will.'

'Don't you mean would?'

'No, I mean will.'

Carly leaned in and planted a gentle kiss on his cheek.

'Oh, don't start with that lovey dovey stuff already,' her mother said, disturbing them.

'Sorry mum, eh I mean Angela.'

Two and a half hours later and the table is strewn with cocktail jugs and glasses all about empty.

Angela squinted to see the time on her watch. 'Oh, our taxi will be coming any minute. He knows not to be late for me. Right, get ready, back to ours to keep the party going.'

'Me too?' Alan asked, praying he was invited.

'Oh, I suppose so,' Angela said, teasing.

They made it out the door as the taxi drew up. 'All in for party town.'

Carly shook her head. 'Think you have drunk enough mum.'

'Okay, mum,' Angela said, then started laughing at her own joke.

At Angela and Carly's house they piled in then lined up for the toilet. Angela first, Alan next followed by Carly and Jason last. When Jason finished, Carly was waiting for him in the lounge.

She gestured to him to sit beside her. They immediately kissed. Jason thought it was the best kiss he had ever had. 'I've been wanting to do that all night.'

'I've wanted it too,' she said, smiling.

They kissed again. And again.

'I was scared you wouldn't like me. The thing is, don't think I am just saying this, but I think I'm falling for you big time.'

'You know, that's exactly the way I feel.'

'What, you thought I wouldn't like you? But why would anybody not like you.'

They were interrupted by a banging from upstairs. They both looked up, as if they would see what was causing it by looking at the ceiling.

'What the Hell is that?'

'Oh, it will be mum and Alan.'

'Doing what?'

The banging continued with a rhythmic thumping.

'You can't guess?'

'You mean they are.'

'Bonking.'

'That's gross. I mean, he is only 22.'

'Oh, she's been with younger than that.'

'No way. Does she do that with everybody she brings back after a night out?'

They are interrupted as the banging gets more rhythmic and noisier.

'Pretty much.'

'What do you do?'

'Oh, I usually listen to music with my earphones on. Try

to blank it out but I still know it's going on.'

'And I moan at my mum that she needs to go out more. Maybe I am lucky she sits in and does word searches and watches Soaps on TV.'

'Oh, if only my mum was like that. She was a bit like that until dad left. I think it's her way of rebelling. Do you want to, you know, go up and do it?'

'Oh, I would like nothing better but not tonight. Not some drunken rumble under the covers.
I think the first time should be special. I want it to be special for you too.'

'That's the nicest thing somebody ever said to me. To be honest I didn't want to do it tonight either but I didn't want you to think I was some kind of prude. Tell you what, mums away on a
course next weekend. You could stay over on Friday. '

'Stay over. That sounds great.' Jason kissed her again. The thought of staying over thrilled him.

Monday morning and Jason and Alan are in the back of the cab. They are both still excited after Friday nights events.

'Hope Angela is up for it again next weekend. Boy, she is something else.'

'No luck. She is at a course all weekend. Carly has the house to herself.'

'We could have a party then. Few mates, drink, some good tunes.'

'Sorry mate, we are having a party for two and you ain't one of the two.'

'Oh, right. So, will you go all the way. Pop your cherry, make the beast with two backs?'

Jason just nodded.

'You should have did it last week, she offered.'

'Look, I wish I hadn't told you. You are right, maybe I should have did it but I shit out of it. Said I didn't believe in sex on the first date. Women appreciate that shit, thought you knew that.'

'Good thinking, man. I will make a shagger of you yet.'

'No, I don't want to be a shagger, I want to be a nice lover.'

'How fucking quaint.'

Lunchtime that day and Jason and Charlie are alone in the van. Charlie calls Jason to slip through to the front seat.

'Right, lad, you are really keen on this girl you're dating.'

'Really keen.'

'Okay, I don't speak much but I hear plenty. These ears aren't painted on. So, all I want to say is be honest. Sure, you might tell little white lies but if you tell them something that might hurt them later, it will backfire on you. That Recycling thing is a load of crap. You are a binman. Tell her you are a binman. If she doesn't want to date a binman, she is not the girl for you. However, if she likes you like you think, she will be happy to date a binman.'

'But Alan says.'

'Alan is a gobshite. Nice enough boy but full of shite. And the only person Alan looks after is himself. Anyway, you never answered, what is wrong with being a binman?'

'Nothing.'

'Exactly. So, remember, the truth, the whole truth and nearly all the truth.'

'Thanks Charlie.'

Friday morning, Charlie and Alan in the bin lorry, Jason is late again.

There is a gentle knocking on the rear passenger door. Alan moves over and looks out.

'It's Jason!' He opens the door but Jase doesn't even move towards the door. Alan jumps out.

'Fuck sake man, you look like death warmed up.'

'I think I've got the flu.'

'Why did you not phone in sick? Jeese oh, you can't empty bins in that state. Charlie, come and see the nick of him.'

Charlie gets out and walks round. He shakes his head when he sees the state he is in.

'Get him in the wagon. We will take him home.'

'No, I can't. I've got a date tonight. Can't be off today.'

Charlie lifted him and bodily sat him in the passenger seat.

'God oh, you are sweating like a gay in a sausage factory. Your only date tonight is with a duvet.'

'Oh, I wish I was dead. Can't even see to text. Alan, will you tell Carly I am ill.'

'I've not got her number but I will phone Angela and explain it all to her. Of all nights, it was cherry popping Friday.'

Jason wanted to tell him to fuck off but only a weak fu came out.

Monday morning saw a newly energised Jason waiting at the lorry. Charlie was next to show.

'You alive! Didn't think we would see you this side of Christmas, if at all.'

'Mum loaded me up with painkillers and other shit. Didn't wake up until yesterday morning at 11 o'clock.'

Alan strolled up to the wagon. He was as shocked as the driver that his workmate had made it.

'Alan, did you tell Carly I was ill? Tried her all afternoon yesterday but she didn't reply then I phoned her and it rang out.'

'Yes, I told her. Angela's phone was going straight to answer machine because she was at that course so I went over to the house personally and I told her.'

'Oh, cheers mate. What did she say?'

'Oh she was really cut up about it. Made you a special meal and everything. It was lovely.'

'You mean you had my dinner!'

'Carly practically begged me to join her. It would have gone to waste, you see, with her mother being away and all. She is a good cook.'

Jason lunged forward and grabbed Alan by the front of his overalls.

'You better not have tried anything or so help you I will kill you.'

Alan raised his arms in capitulation but Jason held tight to his material.

'Steady, Jason. She is your bird. Mates don't nick other mates women.'

Charlie, moving quicker than his bulk should have allowed was out of the cab and separated the two. 'What the Hell is going on here?'

'He is up to something. Nips round to my birds, tells her I am ill then sits down to my dinner. Now she won't answer my texts or calls. Sounds fishy.'

'Does sound a bit fishy,' Charlie agreed, giving Alan the evil eye.

'I will tell you something, Alan, if you have ruined it for me, I will kill you.'

Charlie let go of Jason then pulled Alan round and up until he was on his tip toes and they were face to face. 'And I will help him.'

'Honest, Charlie, Jason, I never laid a finger on her. Man, she is right into you. I don't know why she hasn't contacted you'

Charlie let him down with a final word. 'You better not have.'

Out on the street Jason and Alan are busy emptying the

Recycling boxes into the lorry.

'Alan, phone Angela!'

'I phoned her 10 minutes ago, it's going straight to her machine.'

'Try again.' His tone changed getting angrier and Alan thought he better do as asked to pacify his mate.

'All right, keep your overalls on. If Charlie gets angry, it's on your head.'

Alan rings and Jason stands next to him to hear what she says. On speaker, the ringing tone seemed to go on for ages before Carly's mothers sweet voice came on.

'Hi, it's Angela. Leave a message. If I like you, I will call you back.'

'Leave a message!' Jason ordered. It wasn't a suggestion.

'Hi Angie, it's Alan. You know, from last week. Jason is worried about Carly. Could you get her to phone him or you phone me.'

'Why would Carly phone you?'

'What? No, Carly has to phone you or Angela will phone me. God, you are paranoid.'

'All I am saying is you better not be up to something.'

Lunchtime arrived and still no word. Jason and Charlie are in the cab while Alan is out at the chip shop. Jason decides to look through Alan's backpack. He doesn't know what he is looking for but when he finds his wee book of birds, as he calls it, he decides to look through it.

'Gees, he has been busy. Ashley, 7. Sam. Sam? It must be short for Samantha but with him you never know. Anyway Sam gets a 6.'

Charlie is watching from his mirror. 'Hey, you shouldn't be reading that, it's private. Now, I wouldn't let him go through your stuff so put it back now.'

'He is up to something and I will find out. I mean, I thought it was all talk but this is heavy. Kayla , 8, Megan,8, Kayla 5 and he has put bj in brackets.'

'Come on. Put it back now. Put it back now!'

Before he does, he flicks through to the end of the entries.

'Bastard!, he shouts before throwing the book back in the bag and charging out of the lorry.

Alan was still getting served in the chippy so Jason paces up and down outside waiting.

When Alan walks out, Jason runs up behind him and launches himself onto his back.

They both fall to the ground while Jason keeps a grip round Alan's waist.

'What the fuck! Get off me you mad cunt.'

'What did you do with Carly?'

Alan tries to struggle but is pinned down with Jason's bodyweight.

'Nothing. I never touched her.'

'Well why is her name in your book?'

Before he could answer, Charlie grabbed them both and lifted them right off the ground.

'Right, quit it, you couple of fuds. You have got Charlie angry. You don't want to get Charlie angry.'

He then carried them both by their scruffs to a nearby picnic bench. He let Alan go and told him to sit opposite while Jason was plonked next to him. Charlie put his leg over his and he was anchored by solid muscle.

'Supper,' he said to Alan who laid out his fish and chips.

'Right, Jason, what's eating you?'

'I read his book. The last name in it was Carly's.'

'What are you doing reading my book?'

'Because I knew you were up to something, you dirty rat. Turns out I was right.'

'No. Well, I never did anything to or with Carly.'

'So, why is her name in there?'

Charlie stopped eating. 'Right, Alan. For once I want the truth. I have always known you were a sneaky wee tube, come on, come clean.'

'Okay, hands up. I am a player. Every hole is a goal, that's my motto. When you took ill on Friday I went to Carly's. She invited me to dinner and I thought I could seduce you behind your back.'

Charlie had to steady Jason as he tried to free himself to get at Alan.

'I am going to fucking kill you.'

'No, listen. She made me dinner. We had a drink and I tried it on but she was having none of it. She is right into you man. She really is. So, I really don't know why she hasn't contacted you.'

Jason points over the table. 'I am going to kill you when Charlie lets me loose.'

Charlie pulls his outstretched hand. 'You aren't killing anybody. Not until the end of the shift anyway. After that, well fact is, I might just give you a hand.'

'Hang on Charlie, it's nothing to do with you.'

Charlie's hand was coming round to point to Al just as they were interrupted by Alan's phone ringing.

'Hello.' He nods then hands the phone over to Jason.

'Hello. Oh, hi Angela. Did she? That's exactly what I had. Did she say anything about Alan? Right, okay. Get her to call me. Bye.'

The other two have been staring at him and both say 'Well,' at the same time.

'Carly has been ill since Saturday. She had to go and stay with her gran. She forgot her charger so her battery went flat which was why she couldn't contact me.'

'What's wrong with her?' Alan asked.

'Flu. Sounds like the same thing I had.'

'So, are you two pals again.'

Jason looked at Charlie then Alan.

Alan stuck his hand out. 'Shake?'

'No! I will wait until I talk with Carly first.'

Charlie still hadn't released any pressure on Jason. 'If I release you, you won't do anything silly?'

'No. But I think I will try and get a move to another crew. One I can trust.'

'Don't worry, Jason, if anybody's leaving, it won't be you.'

Friday afternoon and the crew are getting ready for the weekend. Jason has been sitting in the front seat since Chippygate, Alan in the back on his own.

'So, what are your plans for the weekend?' Charlie asked.

'I am going to the pub tonight,' Alan said, leaning forward so as to be heard. 'Probably pick up a couple of birds. Pump the two of them in a threesome no doubt.'

'I wasn't talking to you!' Charlie snapped, cutting him off.

'Charlie, I am going home, showering then going to Carly's for dinner.'

'What have you bought her?'

'Bought her?'

'Come on. You can't turn up for a date without flowers, chocolate or a bottle of nice wine.'

'I didn't know.'

'So much for your dating guru. Right, there is a florist on

the way back to the depot. I will stop for you.'

Jason walked gingerly into the florists. The smell and vast array of flowers overwhelmed him. The assistant flounced round from behind the counter to see him.

'Hi there. How can I help you, sweetie?'

Jason stared at the guy who was openly gay.

'I am looking for a bunch of flowers', he stammered.

'Well, as the boss said to the labourer, take your pick.'

Jason stared at the vast array and different types of bouquets.

'Is it for a lady friend, boyfriend, partner, wife, mother or me?'

'Girlfriend.'

'What a shame. Anyway, you should say it with flowers. What do you want to say?'

'I love you.'

'Oh, such a surprise and we have only met.'

Jason flushed.'Oh, no, not you, Carly.'

'Relax, I was only at the wind-up. Now nothing says I love you more than red roses.'

'How much are they?'

'A dozen red roses are £25. A single red rose will cost a fiver but I will do you 6 for £10.'

'I will take the six, please.'

Jason stood on Carly's doorstep. All sorts of emotion were running through him. Nerves, excitement, joy, fear of disappointment. His hand was shaking a bit as he rang the bell.

Carly opened the door. She was as lovely as he remembered. His smile dropped a bit when he realised she was wearing her housecoat. Was he too early or worse, was she ill again?

'Am I too early?'

'No. Come in.'

She opened the door and let him past her.

'Oh, these are for you,' he said, handing over the roses.

'They are absolutely lovely. Thanks.' She laid them on the floor. 'Right, jacket and shoes off.'

Jason did as he was told. While he was doing this Carly was walking up the stairs.

'Coming up?' she asked before opening her robe to reveal she was naked. 'Well?'

For the first time in his life Jason had an instant hard-on. Indeed he was on the verge of shooting his wad there and then. He ran up the stairs and found Carly lying naked on the top of her bed.

Jason drank in her body, a body he had dreamed about seeing since her very first reply to his

request on the Dating App. Alan was right in that she wasn't one of the skinny things you see that look like they only eat lettuce and drink water. She was more like a burlesque dancer, bumps and curves in all the right places.

While he stood there staring Carly squeezed a breast in each hand seductively. 'What are you waiting for?'

Jason snapped out of his reverie and started ripping his clothes off. In his hurry he managed to get his leg caught in his trousers and fell to the floor with a thump.

Carly burst out laughing.

Downstairs in the kitchen, Angela was preparing dinner and stopped with a jerk when there was a crash above. She looked up and smiled. Carly would be all right.

Somehow Jason retained his stiffy. As he made a bee-line for his girl, she stopped him in his tracks.

'Condom,' Carly whispered, seductively.

'Oh, right,' he said then rummaged in his trousers. Getting the foil pouch out, he struggled to get the packet open then made a face as some of the lub slipped into his mouth.

He turned his back on the bed to prepare himself. When he walked to the side of the bed, Carly burst out laughing.

'Oh my God, that looks like a little bank robber,' she said looking at his penis in it's pink rubber protection.

Jason took it in his hand. 'Open up. This is a stick up. Well, I hope it will be,' he said, pretending it was his penis talking.

Carly managed to stop laughing quickly then lay round on her back. 'Get on with it.'

Jason lay beside her and they kissed. As his hand slip up to caress her left breast Carly whispered that she was ready for him.

Jason was glad Wendy had tutored him. Slowly, he moved between her legs and carefully slipped his covered manhood into her eager vagina.

Once in he started slowly, bringing himself to the brink of slipping out before pushing in as far as he could. His slowness only lasted a short time as the thrill and pleasure he was getting made him go faster. He only realised he would finish long before Carly orgasmed when the headboard started banging against the bedroom wall. Back under control, he managed to continue until everything seemed to get warm in their erogenous zones before emptying himself into the ribbed rubber.

He lay back for a minute to get his breath back then turned to face Carly. She had a little tear in her eye.

'Are you okay? Don't say I hurt you.'

'No. It was my first time. I am just happy. In fact I don't think I have ever been so happy.'

'Mine too,' he lied.

There moment of bliss was disturbed by Angela shouting up that dinner would be on the table in 5 minutes and she would prefer them with their clothes on.

'Is your mum in? Oh my God, she must have heard us.'

'So, I've had to listen to her often enough.'

Getting dressed, Jason turned to his girlfriend. 'You know until two weeks ago if somebody said you could fall in love at first sight I wouldn't have believed them.'

'That's the same way I feel.'

Jason, with only his t-shirt and socks on and with a drooping condom filled with his man milk, got down on one knee.

'Carly, will you marry me?'

STEVEN'S STORY

STEVEN opened the door to the IT office and walked in sheepishly. He had been off work on holiday for a fortnight and he had been dreading this moment more than anything.

The office was laid out with two desks facing each other down one wall with the other other wall being a workshop area with bits of computer, printer and other inter-fazing matter scattered haphazardly.

Seated at the far desk was his mate, Brad who he shared the office with. They are both in their early 40's but Steven wore shirt, tie and flannels whereas Brad tended to put his own spin on smart casual. Today it was faded blue denim shirt and black jeans.

'Well Steven, two weeks off, what or who did you get up to? Plenty of nooky I hope.'

'For God's sake man, let me at least get my computer switched on first.'

Brad drummed his fingers on his desk impatiently until Steven had had enough.

'Right, what?'

'Well, what did you get up to?'

'Nothing.'

'Come on. A fortnight, you must have done something.'

'Ate, shat, slept, that's about it.'

'No pumping?'

'No pumping.'

'Two weeks and not a single shag?'

'As a matter of fact I didn't. I suppose I better tell you know and get it over with. I spent the first week moving from my lovely house to a shitty fucking bedsit. The rest of the time I spent as they say, disentangling myself, from Karen. Karen, the fucking bitch that was my partner for the last 5 years and 4 months. But bitter, no I am not fucking bitter.'

'No way, you and Kaz! Man, I thought you were made for each other. Thought you were real solid.',

'So did I but thanks to Philip Wanking Schofield coming out she decided to come out as a lesbian. Always has been according to her, been in denial. Wish she was in the de fucking Nile right now, right over her head. So she has already moved her other half Cheryl in with her. Bed couldn't even have been cold. Bet my impression was still on the pillow.'

'Holy fucking wank-bags. Karen a rug muncher. Which one is she, the butch or the feminine one?'

'Oh, for fucks sake man. She just broke my heart and you have just ripped it out and stood on it. So, sorry but I don't give a fuck what one she is or who she does now. My only hope is that she gets some very painful, incurable disease preferably sexually related.'

'You are right, man. I was a bit insensitive.'

'A bit! Oh sure, I forgot sensitive is your middle name. Listen, I haven't told anybody else so keep it to yourself. It's not the kind of thing you want broadcast.'

'You are right man. God, that would kill me. Can't think of anything worse, kicking you out for another woman. A right kick in the balls that. Anyway, I will have to tell the wife. I don't mean it like that but you know, Alice and Karen, they got on well.'

'Hopefully not too well.'

'What do you mean?'

'Nothing. Nothing. Anyway, don't make it public.'

Their silent pause is interrupted by the phone ringing. Brad answers.

'IT Department, Brad speaking.' He then nodded sagely as the other person spoke.

'Right, okay. I will reset your password and email your

supervisor a new one. Now this will let you in but then you need to change it.' Brad wrote down details as the other person spoke.

'Oh, Angela, that's a lovely name. You must be new here. I would have remembered that name.'   He then listened again before adding, 'No, it's not Bradley, it's short for Bradford. That's where my parents think I was conceived. They were well ahead of the Beckhams.'

During the call, Steven makes a gagging gesture, to let Brad know his patter was vomit inducing. Brad responded with a two fingered salute.

He laughs and nods again. 'Well I am sure our paths will cross. IT we are a bit like husbands you know, can't live with them, can't live without them. Okay, bye then.'

Steven was shaking his head. 'You never switch off, do you?'

'It's nice to be nice. Anyway, it's you that needs to try the charm offensive.'

'Me? Why?'

'Well, you are over 40, single again and living in a bedsit. Could you be any sadder?'

'Oh yes, kick a man when he is down. Your mates are supposed to rally round and help you when you are at your lowest.'

'Sorry mate, but we have been there for you too often. Tough love, that's what you will be getting from now on. Tell you what, I will act as your official matchmaker. Then I will school you in the art of dating. You can call me your Love Guru.'

'Love Guru. Love fucking Guru. What do you know about dating and matchmaking?'

'Well, I picked my wife and Alice and I have been married for 26 years.'

'Oh right, I will give you that. You are punching well above your weight with Alice.'

'Listen Alice, knows when she is onto a good thing.'

'Oh yes, lucky Alice. Look, leave it just now. I am just getting over this fuck up. I will tell you when I am ready to start dating again. Last thing I need is to get hitched up with another fucking bitch.'

'Up to you man.'

Steven is at home in his bedsit. The furniture came with the flat and was what Steven would call skip chic. It was the kind of stuff that if you put in a skip even the homeless wouldn't take it out.

Steven watches as his microwave dinner turns and cooks. Ting, the microwave the impending arrival of the piping hot Macaroni Cheese.'

He takes it out and looks at it. It looks horrible and smells horrible. He blows on a forkful to cool it then tastes it. It tastes worse than it looks if that was possible. He spits it back onto the tray and drops the lot into the pedal bin.

The fridge is next to the bin. He opens it for something else to eat. In it there is a tin of beans, some milk and a can of beer. He takes the beer and opens it. Sitting on the bed-settee he jumps as a spring pokes through the worn material and nips his arse causing to spill some beer down his white shirt.

How did life take me to this, he mused. Fucking lezzie Karen that was how.

Brad was sitting at home on his comfy armchair relaxing with a glass of beer. The TV is on with some banal comedy that is failing to entertain. Alice is sprawled on the settee sipping at a gin and tonic.

'Oh, here, I have something to tell you. Wait 'till you hear this. Steven and Karen have split up. And get this, Karen is with another woman.'

'Oh Brad, I thought you were going to tell me something.'

'What, you knew?'

'Well, it was all over her Facebook page two weeks ago.'

'Her Facebook! Oh my God. Steven wants to keep it quiet and it's been all over Facebook for weeks. So, why did you not tell me?'

'Well you call it Two-faced book and always say you don't

want to know anything about it.

Not that you ever listen to anything I have to say. Are you saying now you want us to sit and talk about things.'

'But Steven and Karen, they were so solid.'

'Well, I had my doubts.'

'How come?'

'It was that time when we were all at the Spa together. Remember, about 2 years ago. Well, she said I had nice tits.'

'No way. Wow! Just like that, I like your tits.'

'No, not just like that. We were in the jacuzzi. We had a few glasses of bubbly. We were the only two in the tub and she just took off her bikini top. Her tits were quite small and her nipples were inverted.'

'Inverted? What do you mean?'

'They curve in the way. Anyway, at first I was a wee bit embarrassed but I joined her. Whipped my top off.'

'You never, ever told me about that.'

'Anyway, she said I had nice tits. Said they were perfect and she wished hers were like mine. Then she said do you mind if I touch them then she reached over and fondled them.'

'Oh my God. You just sat there and let her.'

'Why not? After a bottle of Prosecco, anything goes. Anyway, she knew how to rub them seductively.'

'Were you turned on?'

'Too right. But not in a lesbian way. I jumped on you that night. Twice we did it. Or was it three times?'

'Oh yes, I remember. I just thought it was just the drink. So, do you think you will be turned on tonight?'

'I might be. I will need to see if I have Karen's number.'

Next morning, Steven is at his desk first. Brad was hardly in the door when Steven ushered him to sit down.

'Right, mate. Sit down. I have had enough of the single life. I need more.'

'No, you probably just need sex. Right, I will need the morning to think about it. We will discuss it in the pub at lunchtime.'

Steven is sitting in a stall in the bar of their usual lunch-time haunt. Brad walks over with a tray with pints and sandwiches. The pub was quite busy with lunch-time drinkers and diners.

'Hey, you should be buying the drinks. After all, I am doing you the service.'

'You haven't done anything yet.'

'That's where you are wrong. I have been thinking of where you are going wrong. Lets start with your image.'

'What's wrong with my image?'

'What's right with it? Okay, I am going to be honest with you because that's what Love Guru's do. You are grey. Everything about you is grey. Dull and boring. You wear the same boring clothes, get the same boring haircut and do the same boring things. Dull and boring. Sorry mate but that is the honest truth.'

Steven looked down at himself. White shirt, grey tie, black flannels and shiny, black dress shoes. He tried to think about a come-back but for once his mate was right. He looked at his mate. He was wearing a fancy light blue shirt of a style that was trendy in the 70's and 80's, dark grey trousers which were slightly flared and desert boots.

'So, what do you think, I should dress more like you? You know, sort of washed up 70's throwback?'

'Steven, you are not cool enough to carry this look off.'

'Yes and neither are you.'

'Sense a wee bit of jealousy there. Right, I will give you another example. Give me one of your business cards.'

Steve opened his wallet and retrieved a card.

Brad looks at it and places it on the table. 'Steven Harvey IT. The Sand H are capitals so it spells out SHIT! That just about sums you up at the minute matey.'

'Glad you are making me feel better. So I am a dull and boring shit.'

'Good. First thing you had to do is realise you were going

at life the wrong way. So next we re-image you. You will feel like a new man. Ready to take on the dating game and woman on your terms. Right, first thing is your name.'

'Wow, I am not changing my name.'

'Okay, just hear me out. Steven. When you hear Steven you think of a young guy. You know, is Steven coming out to play? Or an old guy. That's Steven passed away. Mind you he was 82. You are a forty-something guy who wants to be hip and trendy which you can be, with my help, of course. So your options are Steve, Stevie or Stevo.'

'I am not going round getting called Stevo you can cut that crap right now.'

'Right. Hold on. Ladies!'

Two woman, in their twenties are at the bar. Just drinking, not eating, obviously not office workers in for lunch. When they turn round it is plain to see one of them has had more to drink than she probably should.

'Have you got a wee second?'

They totter over to their table.

'This is my friend. He is having a bit of an identity crisis. Could you answer a wee question, what name do you think suits him, Steven, Steve or Stevie?'

The first girl, the sober one, says, 'Stevie. I think Stevie suits you.'

The other one looks him up and down although obviously struggling to focus. 'Steven because you look like a boring bastard.' Laughing to herself, she turns and totters back to her drink.

Her friend is embarrassed by her drunk mate. 'Sorry about that, she just found out her boyfriend is leaving her.'

'Oh, shame. Hope it wasn't for another man,' Brad said, much to Steve's ire.

'No, her sister.'

The lads look at each other then in unison say, 'Dirty bastard.'

The girl agrees with them then leaves to try to console her

pal.

'Missed a chance there, Steve. She is single again.'

'Sod off. She was young enough to be my daughter and she obviously has a drink problem.

Oh, and don't forget she said I was a boring bastard. Cheeky cow! There again you couldn't resist getting a dig in. Hope it's not with another guy. You know you can be a right prick at times.'

'Settled one thing, though. The word in the street is Stevie.'

'Well, it's not exactly the street. Two lassies in a pub isn't a straw poll but now I think about it, I do like Stevie. Hi there, I'm Stevie. Does make me sound more interesting.'

'Right, plan is Saturday you get down the High Street and get yourself some new duds.

Do you want me to come with you, give you a few fashion tips.'

'No. Definitely not.'

'Next, what do you think about coming down the gym with me for a few sessions?'

'I think I would rather stick knitting needles in my eyes.'

'I will take that as a maybe just now. The thing is, you know, it takes a bit of effort to keep a body as trim as this.'

'So how come you have a bit of a belly?'

'That's the fuel tank for the sex machine. Okay then, it's something to think about. So, this afternoon we set you up on a dating site.'

Stevie and Brad are at there desks. Brad had been ribbing him since they came back, calling him different names every time he wanted him for something. Eventually Stevie cracked.

'Right, cut the crack. We will stick with Stevie and that's an end to it!'

'Fair enough. Right give me your phone over.'

'Why, can I not operate my own phone?'

'No, but these Dating Sites can be a bit awkward to set up.'

'I am still not sure I should trust you with my love life.'

'Look, I set up 3 of Alice's mates and they are all happily loved up now, all thanks to the Love Guru. With your track record I wouldn't trust you with your sex life. Okay, the website the girls all used is called Kissing Frogs. No kissing of amphibians is required and it's free. No charge whatsoever. Firstly full name.'

'Steven Harvey, no middle name.'

'Steven. Come on, Stevie boy, stick with the program or it won't work.'

'Sorry, Brad. Only been Stevie for an hour and it's taking a bit of getting used to.'

'Right, favourite food?'

'Steak.'

'Good, he-man, meat-eater and it should deter the Vegan's. You don't want another Vegan.'

'No I fucking don't. Karen was a lesson never to be repeated.'

'God I just realised, that was why she didn't like your meat, her being a Vegan Lesbian. Right, fave drink?'

'Red wine.'

'No, not just red wine. You need to embellish it. I will say claret. Favourite film?'

'The Wizard of Oz.'

'Are you pulling my plonker? Do you want folk to think you are a friend of Dorothy's?'

'I thought with these Apps the most important thing was honesty?'

'Oh sure, but in your case honestly would probably get you a female version of yourself. I for one don't want to ever meet a female you and I don't think you would either.'

'Okay then, my next best is Chitty Chitty Bang Bang. I loved that film as a kid.'

'I saw the porn version of that, Pretty Shitty Gang Bang.'

'Don't put that down, don't want to be some kind of perve like you.'

Brad keeps laughing to himself. 'Pretty shitty gang bang. Good film too. Anyway, you do understand you can pick adult films too. You know, grown up films.'

'You asked for my favourite film.'

'Right, I will put that down. Your choice. Favourite film star?'

'George Clooney.'

'Good choice. Liked by woman of all ages, clean cut, family man. Yes, really good choice.'

'No, I just like his films.'

'Sorry, I thought you were taking this seriously. Next, favourite TV show.'

'The Chase.'

'Okay, bit of a thinker. Right, I will fill the rest of this in myself.'

'Wow! You can't say I'm not taking this seriously then not let me give me your views.'

'Right, okay. Next then, favourite colour?'

'Haven't really got a favourite colour.'

'Everybody has got a favourite colour. What about green?'

'That's fine.'

'Occupation. Right, you have a lot of choice here.'

'IT worker.'

'IT worker. Come on, where's your imagination. Think of the scope you have,
IT Consultant, IT Manager, IT Expert, IT Specialist.'

'What do you think would be best?'

'IT Manager sounds best. Most gravitas. Even though you only manage yourself.'

'Right, IT Manager it is.'

'Favourite singer?'

'Elton John.'

Brad shakes his head. 'Friend of Dorothy.'

'George Michael.'

More head shaking. 'Dorothy.'

'What about Queen?'

'Well Freddy's was one of Dorothy's besties but everybody likes a bit of Queen. Favourite song?'

'Don't stop me now.'

'That's okay as long as you don't sing it while you are making out.'

'Making out? Making out? What fucking age are you?'

'So, what would you call it?'

'Snogging.'

'Oh well, that is so much more mature. Right, last question, favourite season?'

'Autumn. Walks in the crisp morning frost. The leaves on the trees turning brown.'

'Fuck me, it's not an episode of Countryfile. Anyway, we are done.'

'I think I have been.'

Steve walks into the office to find Brad, at his desk and smiling like a Cheshire cat.

'The results are in lad and they ain't bad.'

'What results?'

'The Dating App.'

Stevie walks round to Brad's computer screen.

'Is that my Dating App page you are looking at?'

'Well, yes. Part of my role as Love Guru. God some of them are hot totty.'

'Never mind that, how did you get into that?'

'Well, I set it up for you. I am a computer geek, you don't need to be Einstein to work that out. You used the password you always use. Sit round here and browse. That way if anybody comes in they won't know we are browsing.'

'You will get us hung.'

'You would be first sacked, seeing as you are the manager after all. Right, I've got it down to 3.'

'Hold on, I read up on it last night, the best fit for a partner is the first one on the list.'

'That's the theory but your ideal match is Lucy.'

'She looks nice.'

'Nice. Nice. I want more than nice for you. Steven would have been happy with nice but Stevie deserves better.'

'So, what's wrong with Lucy then?'

'Too homely, makes her own clothes, drives a wee puddle-jumper car. Makes love under the covers with the light off.'

'It says that all in there?'

'No, that's the Love Guru's view because I can read women. You will find out I am right.'

'So, what is your choice oh Mystic one?'

'First Grace.'

'Okay, I will give you that, looks pumpable.'

'Grace. Likes fine food, keen walker, drives a beemer, loves experimenting in the bedroom and I don't mean with a Chemistry set.'

'Your opinion?'

'Not an opinion, you will find out I am about 90% right.'

'Only 90%. Right, number 2.'

'Kate. Very romantic, loves weddings. That's a hint she wants to settle down. Drives a Corsa, goes like a train if she finds the right guy and that could very well be you, with, of course my help. Third and certainly not least is Shirley. Look at the jugs on her, she could feed triplets with those mamma's.'

'How, has she got three tits?'

'No but she is certainly well stacked.'

'Oh, I like a big breast but not big bouncy things like those.'

'Oh man, would you not go out with her just so you could tell me about it. I've always dreamed about playing with a pair of jugglies like them.'

'Sorry pal but it's Grace or Kate.'

'Stevie, with my schooling it will be a penalty kick.'

'You were always crap at football.'

Brad looked at Alice over the dining table. 'Your hair looks nice, have you done something too it?'

'Yes, I have combed it.'

'It just looks a bit different.'

'No.'

'No what?'

'You are looking for a jump tonight and the answer is no.'

'I cannot win. Just last week you said I never said anything nice. When I try it, you think I am after the one thing.'

'Oh, so you aren't after a jump?'

'Well, if it is on offer, you know, I will never knock you back.'

'What about the other thing, you know about us talking?'

'Well, my news is that Stevie's got a date tonight.'

'Steven from work, you mean.'

'Yes but he is calling himself Stevie now. It's part of his new image I am working on with him.'

'He is listening to your advice about something,' Alice says, stifling a laugh as she says it.

'We have been on a Dating App and I have been advising him on dating. I am his official matchmaker.'

Alice bursts out laughing.

'It's not funny. In fact he calls me his Love Guru.'

Alice's laugh becomes hysterical. Tears are running down her face. 'Stop, stop. Enough, oh I haven't laughed so much in years.'

Brad folds his arms in frustration.

'Look, if you make me laugh any more I will need to change my Tena.'

'You use those pad things?'

'We are all getting older, things don't work the way they did years ago. We all get slips and drips. Right, I have calmed down enough now. So, what qualifies you to be a Love Guru?'

'You seem to forget I set up three of your friends with their partners.'

'Kirsty, Carol and Mandy?'

'Yes.'

'Kirsty split up with Martin after 3 months because he was addicted to Granny Porn. Carol had a lesbian stalker who she had to get a restraining order for and Mandy's boyfriend moved in with her mother last month.'

'Not my fault they can't hang on to their men. You forget my coup de eh piece de resistance, you.'

'What about me?'

'Well, I chose you.'

'You have a short memory. It might have been 20 years ago but the truth is, I picked you.'

'No, we were in a club. I spotted you across the room and it was love at first sight.'

Alice laughs again but gently this time.

'We were in a club, yes. I was there with my friend Cathy. You had to get drunk to pluck up the courage to come over to talk to us. You got Cathy up to dance and half way round the dance floor you told her you loved her. She signalled me to save her. I took over and rescued her from your clutches. I took you home that night and after that you were mine. So, it was me that picked you.'

Brad stared at his wine glass, gently swirling what was left.

'Do you want some more wine?'

' Yes please. So, who is the lucky lady?'

'You. If you play your cards right.'

'No, dumbo. Who is Steve's lucky lady.'

'She is called Grace. Attractive, dark hair, likes fine dining and walking. Think she is the executive type who drives a sports car.'

'No, that's not the type he needs. She sounds a bit like Karen. No, what he needs right now is a homely type. Possibly a single mum who can mother him a bit, that's what he will need right now.'

'Well, that's your opinion but I think we will find out that I know better.'

Stevie parked his car outside Grace's house. He couldn't wait to see the back of her. The date had been, in his eyes, a complete disaster.

Grace turned and looked seductively at Stevie.

'Thanks for a lovely evening. I feel sorry that you weren't drinking, you may have loosened up a bit. Do you want to come in for coffee?'

'No, I would love to but I have work to do at home then I have to be up really early in the morning.' Stevie wondered if his nose was getting bigger, he was never good at lying.

'Maybe next time. Could I ask you a big, massive favour? I had a break-in last year and I am scared to come back to my house after dark in case it's happened again.'

'Okay, but I really can't wait.'

They got out of the car, Grace leading and Stevie keeping a safe distance behind.

Grace checked each room while Stevie stood in the hallway, ready to make his escape. Survey complete, Grace walked over and got between Stevie and his escape route through the front door.

'Thanks again for a lovely evening.' She leaned forward and kissed him. Her left arm went round his neck until it was almost into a headlock, while her other hand reached down and rubbed enthusiastically at his genitals.

'Look, Stevie, I don't usually do this on a first date but I really like you. Will you come to bed with me?' She whispered in his ear. Seemed strange as they were the only 2 people in the house.

Stevie could feel his heart thumping in his chest. How was he going to get out of this one?

'I will need to go to the car to get condoms.'

'It's okay, I have a selection. I prefer the ribbed, more pleasure.'

'Do you have extra large?'

'Oh, no. Well, hurry back big boy.'

Stevie walks quickly back to the car. He jumped in and drove off without looking back.

Next morning, Stevie walks into the office and slams the door behind him.

'Wow Stevie boy, cool the jets. What's up, date not go to plan?'

'Oh yes Love Guru, you got it right, into fine dining and walking you said.'

'Was I right then?'

'Oh yes, if your interpretation of that was walking from the couch to the fridge and gorging herself. That's the only walking she does.'

'Was she big?'

'Was she big?'

'She was really big then? Didn't look big in the photo.'

'The photo was about 10 years old. And big. When she got in my car it dropped about 6 inches on that side. I nearly ended up in the passenger seat next to her. Four days I wasted texting her and not once did she even hint that she was a heifer. I mean I don't like skinny women, I like them with a bit of beef on the bone but she abuses the privilege. Her dating picture must have been taken about 6 stone ago and even then it must have been Photoshopped. All through the date she could hardly talk for eating then she had the cheek to ask me in for coffee. Then, all meekly she asks me to have sex with her. Oh, I don't usually do this on a first date. My arse, probably shags for food which is why she is so big.'

'You didn't pump her then?'

'No fucking way. The only way we would have had sex would be if I drank that date rape stuff. So she tricked me into the house and grabbed me and kissed me. God, it was awful. Do you remember the scene in Alien when the monster latches onto the victim's face and rams something down his throat? Well that was what a kiss was like from her, her tongue whapping about in my mouth then sliding down my throat. If it wasn't bad enough she had been eating garlic.'

'You could smell it?'

'No, I could fucking taste it. All the time she was probing my mouth her hand was rummaging about with my meat and two veg.'

'Do you think she wanted to eat them too?'

'Well, she didn't get a chance. I made a hasty retreat but I had to lie to her to get out?'

'What did you say, you forgot you were gay?'

'I am not telling you but your reign as Love Guru is over. I am not listening to you any more.'

'Can't believe you. Not had sex in what, 6 weeks?'

'More like 8.'

'I get you it offered on a plate and you knock it back. I would just have pumped her. The fat and ugly ones need pumping too.'

'Well I will give you her number if you want it. She would suck you in and blow you out.'

'What a way to go. Come on, one more go. Kate's next. You know I showed the girls to Alice last night and she reckons Kate would be your best bet.'

'I still think Lucy would be ideal.'

'She reckons the same as me, that Lucy is too homely. You don't want somebody that knits you jumpers, do you?'

'Right, this is your last chance. Kate it is.'

Stevie decided meeting for a first date in a restaurant wasn't a good idea. So next date was in a pub in the city. He sat at the bar with a bottle of beer. In the glass behind the gantry he saw a woman in white approaching him. She was very attractive and as he turned he fixed a big smile.

Kate gets closer and it was no secret from the bump in her front she was about 5 months pregnant.

'Hi, I'm Kate.'

Brad is working on a computer tower while Stevie quietly lets himself into the office. He then slams the door even harder than he did after his last date.

'Fuck me man, I nearly shit myself!'

'Oh, did you get a wee surprise. Sometimes a wee surprise is a good thing. Sometimes it's fucking not.'

'Has this got something to do with your date?'

'Yes, this has got everything to do with my date. Kate. Lovely Kate. Turned up dressed in virginal white. You were right, keen to get married. Kids too, wanting to start a family. What you didn't know was she was that keen she had already started.'

'You mean she was a bit pregnant.'

'You cannot get a bit pregnant, you either are or you aren't and she most definitely was. About 5 or 6 months judging by the size of her.'

'No way. You are kidding me, right?'

'I am not kidding.'

'Did you bang her?'

'No I did not bang her. No way man. That would have been sick.'

'I would have, I have always wanted to bang a pregnant woman. Safest sex ever. I mean you cannot get her up the duff if she already is.'

'Wait a minute. You have two kids. Are you saying you never had sex all the time Alice was pregnant'

'No, we couldn't. Her sister had complications and she was terrified that if we had sex it would harm the unborn baby.'

'And all that time you were bragging about all the sex you were getting. Sex every night you said, couldn't get enough of it. Her hormones were all over the place you said. Couldn't keep her hands off you.'

'Well, if I told you the truth you would have thought less of me.'

'No I wouldn't. That's just you all over, Mister Ego. How you look, how you come across. Nobody really gives a shit about all that man, it's what's in your heart that matters. Take this Love Guru. Think you know everything about dating because you got lucky and met a wonderful woman. You know man, you are so full of shit you should moo.'

'Funnily enough, I saw another girl I thought would be ideal.'

'No, the Love Guru has been sacked. Made redundant. Oh and by the way, I have changed my password to Kissing Frogs so no more spying on my App.'

'Look mate, I was only trying to help.'

'Yes and look where your help has got me. An obese sex maniac and a pregnant woman. '

Lunchtime in the pub and Stevie has cooled a bit. Brad brings over the drinks and sandwiches.

'It was my turn to buy today.'

'These are on me.'

'What are you after?'

'Nothing, these are by way of a wee sorry.'

'You aren't actually going to admit you were wrong?'

'I won't go that far. Anyway, I was looking for a wee favour.'

'No. Whatever it is, the answer is no.'

They eat and drink in silence.

'Would you not even consider.'

'N fucking-o. No!'

'Shirley is my dream woman. Would you not even consider going on one date with her.'

'I thought Alice was your dream woman?'

'Yes she is. Well, Shirley is more my fantasy woman.'

Stevie's phone pings. He looks at it then stares at Brad.

'Did you set this up?'

'What?'

'I have just had a ping from Shirley.'

'How could I do anything, you changed your password?'

'I still think you are up to something?'

'Scouts Honour.'

'You weren't in the Scouts, you were in the Boys Brigade.'

'Well they didn't have B.B.'s honour so I just said Scouts Honour. Honest man, this is nothing to do with me. It's fate. What do you call it, Kermit?'

'Kismet.'

'Surely if it's to do with frogs it will be Kermit. Anyway, this is a sign.'

'Don't give me that sad eyes look. There must be something wrong with her. Midget or hunchback. After the way my luck has been going she will be both.'

Brad continues with the puppy dog eyes.

'Right one date. Then I take over my own destiny.'

Stevie accepts the request and it pings back immediately.

'She seems keen.'

'She has two tickets for the International Film Cinema tomorrow night. I don't like films with subtitles.'

'Come on son, you don't go to the pictures on a date to watch the film.'

'Brad, we are not teenagers. You go to see International Films for the culture. Tell you what, I am taking her for a coffee first. That way if she is wonky I will disappear before we get to the Cinema.'

Stevie stirred at his coffee. He picked a seat facing the front door so that he could see Shirley approach. Just as he took a sip, the coffee shop door opened and Shirley appeared. Stevie nearly choked on the vision. She was drop dead gorgeous. Sure her chest looked big but only because she was stick thin. Now Stevie admitted to himself that although he preferred women of a bit more substance he had been blown away by Shirley's all round beauty.

'Coffee?'

'Could I just get a bottle of water?'

'Sure.' Stevie almost fell over his chair in his hurry to get to the counter.

When he returned to the table, Shirley had made herself comfortable.

'You might think this is a strange question, especially as we have just met but did somebody put you up to asking me out tonight?'

Shirley looked at him as if uncomprehending the question.

'What do you mean?'

'Well my mate, actually he's my workmate, is supposed to be schooling me in the art of dating. He was always saying I should date you but I didn't want to.'

'Why?'

Time for some more quick thinking on Stevie's part.

'To be honest, I thought you were way out of my league.'

'What? No, you are a good looking guy.'

'So, nobody suggested you take me out tonight?'

'No. I had a spare ticket for tonight and when I checked my App, you were the dishiest.'

'Dishy, I don't think I have ever been called dishy.' He felt his cheeks redden.

Shirley opened the bottle of water and took a drink. Stevie couldn't believe somebody taking a drink could look sexy but she pulled it off.

'So, what is it about foreign cinema you like?'

'Oh, it's the French voice?'

'Does it, you know, get you going?' Stevie asked in probably the worst French accent ever attempted.

'Oh yes. When Mr Jones our French teacher used to talk to the class I would get wet.'

There was an awkward silence between them.

'Are you sure it wasn't just Mr Jones' voice that did it?'

'No, I have been to see French films before and always leave a quivering wreck.'

Stevie knew one thing, whatever else, it was going to be an interesting evening.

Inside the theatre foyer, Stevie offered to get the popcorn.

'Sweet or salty,' he asked innocently.

'I prefer something salty in my mouth,' she said with a cheeky grin, then licked her lips seductively.

Popcorn in hand, they headed through to the show.

The usher tried to find them a seat but Shirley told him they would sit up the back. They moved along to near the end of the row, furthest from the aisle.

When his eyes settled to the near dark, Stevie suddenly realised Shirley was the only woman in the audience of about 50 people.

'Shirley,' he whispered, 'What is the name of the film?'

She switched on her phone light to check her ticket. 'Le plombier de passione.'

Although it was 20 odd years since he had studied French, Stevie would guess it was about a passionate plumber. It finally dawned on him he was in a mucky film picture house.

Shirley leaned over and whispered in Stevie's ear. 'Lets play film actions.'

'What's that?' he asked with impending dread.

'Whatever action happens on screen, we do.'

'What do you mean?' although he was sure he knew exactly what it meant.

'Well, whatever the principal actors do on screen, we copy. So, if they kiss, we kiss.'

'I am not sure. I mean, what if they do more than kiss?'

'Well, then it gets interesting.'

As Stevie was working on an excuse in his mind, Shirley leaned in and put her tongue delicately and most provocatively in his ear. His resolve melted. She was as horny as she was pretty.

Shirley cuddled closely as the film started.

On screen, the heroine is at the kitchen sink. As she turns the tap no water comes out.

She turns to face the camera. She is tall and blond and wearing only a thin housecoat and beneath it a hint of black basque and suspenders. Her bulging chest is making an attempt to spill out of the top of her underwear.

'I need a plumber,' is shown in subtitles. The cuddling couple at the back were probably the only two concentrating on the words. Every other eye was straining on the bubbly blond.

'How much,' she says into the phone. 'Two hundred euro.' She looks into her purse, she has fifty euros.

The plumber arrives. He is a strapping Adonis of a man. He is wearing bib and brace and appears to have nothing else underneath.

The plumber lies on the floor with his head and shoulders beneath the sink. As he rummages our heroine slips off a shoe and starts rubbing at his midriff with the sole of her foot.

Next thing Stevie knows is Shirley has managed to get her foot up into his groin and is somehow managing to massage him to a bit of stiffness through his trousers.

The plumber then gets up. The blond shows the contents of her purse then slips a boob out of her basque. The plumber massages the customer's glorious orb.

Without speaking, Shirley takes Stevie's hand and put it in her blouse. Automatically, Stevie massages the big breast and feels the nipple stiffen to his touch.

The plumber then takes the woman in his arms and kisses her.

Stevie takes the lead and takes Shirley in his arms and kisses her. Although both are concentrating on the tongue action Shirley manages to keep an eye on the screen action.

The plumber then loosens the top of his overalls and they fall at his feet. He is naked beneath. Blondie grabs a hold of his manhood and starts rubbing it.

Shirley copies, breaking off from kissing then opening Stevie's trousers and started rubbing expertly.

To start with Stevie was mortified and looked around to make sure nobody was watching them. Stevie's breathing got shallow as he forgot where he was and was lost in the moment. He was getting close to finishing. The spell broken with a torch being shone in their faces.

'What's going on there?'

Stevie, in a bid to save his dignity, rams the popcorn tub over his manhood just as he erupts into it.

The usher then shines the torch at their waists and realises what had been going on.

'I'm going for the manager,' he says, 'You two are going out.' With that he left.

Stevie drops the sloppy contents of the popcorn tub on

the floor and buttons up his fly.

'Better leave before we are thrown out.'

Shirley puts her jacket on and they make their escape.

Out in the fresh air of the night, and far enough away from the doors as to not be followed, the couple burst out laughing then they kiss again.

'Are we going back to mine and we can finish off what we started.'

'Try and stop me,' Stevie said. He had never had an adventure like this.

In the office the next morning, Brad is at the worktop, repairing a laptop. Stevie enters quietly.

'You're late.'

'Don't start. Do not start this morning.'

'Not another disaster?'

'No, quite the opposite. Boy was that girl beautiful but man and she was insatiable.'

'No!'

'Yes!'

'Right, details. Dish the dirt.'

'Well, turns out the International Cinema was actually a wanking picture Palace. Shirley was the only woman in the place. The rest were all the dirty raincoat brigade. So when the film starts we get a bit carried away. The upshot being we decided to leave before we were asked to leave.'

'So, did this involve any nudity?'

'Not really.'

'Details.'

'She had my todger out and was rubbing it. She was very good at it.'

'So, you were caught with your todger out.'

'Well not really. The usher shone his torch on my face so to hide my embarrassment I stuck my tub of popcorn on it but I think from my expression he knew what had just happened.'

'What had happen, oh God, you came into the popcorn tub!'

'This goes nowhere. You tell no-one.'

Brad couldn't have told anyone at that moment as he was doubled up, creased in laughter.

'It's not funny. Well, I suppose it is. Jees, I wonder what the cleaner thought when they found the congealed tub of popcorn this morning. Brad, it's not that funny.'

Brad looked up through tear-filled eyes. He pretended he was re-enacting his version of the previous nights events with an invisible tub.

Although he tried not to, Stevie joined in.

It was five minutes before any sanity returned.

'Right, what happened next?'

'The only way I tell you any more is if you promise popcorn-gate is kept a secret between us.'

'Promise.'

'Okay, here is the deal. If you tell anyone, I tell Alice I only went with Shirley because she was your fantasy woman.'

'Alice wouldn't believe you. No she would. Okay, deal.'

'Right, so we go back to hers. I go and get washed up and get the rest of the popcorn out of my briefs. When I come out she is sitting up on the settee wearing only a black silk kimono. She opened it slightly and showed she had nothing else on. Then she got up and led my by the hand through to the bedroom. She threw the kimono off and lay on the bed. I have never undressed so quickly in my life. The rest, well, we both know what was next.'

'What, that's all you are giving me?'

'To tell you the truth, for all she was gorgeous and had a dream body, when we were doing it, she just lay there. I had my fun though.'

'And that was it? I thought you said she was insatiable.'

'Afterwards we fell asleep in each others arms. I woke up about 4 hours later and she was on top of me. She had somehow got me hard and impaled herself. I just lay there and let her have her fun. She had great technique, never once did I pop out.'

'She did it to you. What about her breasts? You haven't mentioned them.'

'Oh, they were big and soft. Definitely natural and tiny hard nipples when she was aroused.'

'Wow. What a night, eh?'

'That wasn't it over. I woke about six o'clock. Her arm was over my chest and I managed to lift it without waking her. I slid off the bed and crept round the room gathering my clothes. I just got my hand on the door handle when Shirley said, Morning. I turned and she was lying spread-eagled on the bed.'

Stevie paused after this, frustrating his mate.

'Well, what happened next?'

'What do you think? I went back to her. This time it was so different. We caressed and sort of gently made love. It was so natural and we came together. It wasn't frantic, just gentle and slow and it was probably the sweetest love making I have ever had.'

'So, she could be the one?'

'Fuck no! I would be dead within a fortnight.'

'Right, but what a fortnight, eh.'

Lunchtime and they two are in the boozer.

Stevie is at the bar getting the drinks.

Brad shouts over, 'Do they sell popcorn?'

Stevie gave Brad a look. Brad put his hands up as in surrender.

Stevie laid down the drinks. 'Need to go to the toilet.'

'Again? Have you got something wrong?'

'Hope not?'

When Stevie came back he leaned in and whispered to his mate. 'Have you ever had an

STD ?'

'No. How, did you not use condoms?'

'No.'

'You fucking idiot. Oh God, man. It's the first rule!'

'I know. I don't know why, I just got carried away.'

'Right, what are your symptoms?'

'Well, I keep running to the toilet and the end of my willie is sore and feels inflamed.'

'Why don't you go and see the Nurse at work?'

'Sandra Morton? God, no. No way am I showing her my todger. Anyway, she isn't a real Nurse, she is a Wages Clerk.'

'Oh and if you had a heart attack or stroke and she came running to help are you going to lie there, preparing for your last breath and saying- sorry Sandra, you ain't a real Nurse. She is a fully trained Emergency Responder.

'This isn't an emergency.'

'I don't know, what if your todger falls of or rots away and the Doctor says, why did you not come to me sooner.'

'I will phone the local Health Centre when we get back in the office. Anyway, Sandra's days of running to an emergency are long gone. Last running she ran to a bell it was the dinner bell at school.'

'That's true. Still, she might not know much about STDs but I'm sure she would give the wee fellow a good looking at.'

'Thanks, but I will leave it to the professionals.'

Next morning and Stevie enters the office later than usual and is very sheepish.

'What did the Doctor say, does it have to come off?'

'No.'

'Come on, spill the beans.'

'Right I went in and described the symptoms to the Doctor. He was saying things like no discharge, itching, blood coming out. Then he asked when I last have sex. So I said the other night and we had it three times. He went mental. Here is me, a successful Doctor he went on, beautiful wife, lovely house, fancy car and he gets sex once a month. Then he says it's not as if I was even a good looker. I said I hadn't asked for a second opinion but the humour was wasted on him. So then he said we will need to see the little chap. When he said we I thought he was going to call in other Doctors or students. Lucky for me it was just his way of talking. So I am up on the table, trousers at my ankles and he puts his gloves on and has a good look at him. Then he gets in close and for a minute I thought he was going to suck it but he just smelt it. Then he ran his fingers up the shaft. He rubbed on a slight lump I hadn't noticed. Then he peeled back my foreskin, right back it went. Then he asked me if I had been having anal sex.'

'Did you? You and Shirley?'

'No. Anyway he plucks something off the inside of my foreskin and says here's the culprit here. Looks like a bit of corn, he says. Turned out to be a bit of uncooked popcorn.'

Stevie hears a crash and looks round to see Brad on the floor. He runs round to his mate's aid only to find him convulsed in laughter.

'Oh, it's fucking funny. Well, when you recover from this fit, I have news for the Love Guru. You are sacked. I have been accosted, compromised by a pregnant woman and sexually abused by a nymphomaniac. In fact, from now on I am going celibate.'

Brad managed to stop laughing to say- 'Sell a bit- you can't even give it away.'

'Very bloody funny but I mean it. Dating no more! And another thing, not a word about this, not even to Alice. I mean it, breath a word of it and she finds out what happened at last years Christmas party.'

'You wouldn't. You promised.'

'Up until now I haven't breathed a word about it. This is on a par.'

'Okay, not a word.'

'To anybody, even Alice.'

'To anybody, even Alice.'

'Stevie, it's been two weeks mate. Try another go at the Dating App. You have been so miserable. At least if you had a woman you could be the same miserable as the rest of us.'

'What, you get different kinds of miserable?'

'Oh, yes. Tell you what, why don't you, me and Alice hit the town on Friday night. Alice can try and help you pick up a woman.'

'She'll be better at it than you. It would be hard not to be.'

Brad and Alice were already seated when Stevie entered the nightclub. It wasn't a thumpy music kinda place. More decent background music, posh décor, intelligent talk and expensive drink.

Alice moved over and motioned for Stevie to sit next to him. Alice looked gorgeous as ever. She probably took a while to look as if she hadn't spent any time to look stunning.

'Sit with me, Stevie. Now before you start, no corny jokes.'

Stevie gave Brad the evil look, he better not have told Alice. Brad, in absolute panic, nodded as if to deny any knowledge.

'Get Stevie a drink while I talk to him.'

Brad went over to the bar but realised when he put a hand on the bar to found it was shaking. He looked back at Stevie and Alice, they were chatting away, he just hoped he believed the corn story wasn't the topic of conversation.

'So, Brad says you have given up on women?'

'After his help? Has he told me about my eh adventures?'

'Bits and pieces. I told him you need somebody homely. A house-maker, somebody who wants a family. You need to settle down.'

'You know, you are probably right. Brad wants me to go with these ravers while I just want a quiet life.'

'Right, give me your phone, show me your Dating App.'

Stevie takes out his phone and finds the App.

'Lucy. She seems ideal. I take it you don't fancy her.'

'She was my first choice but Brad said she was too homely. Makes her own clothes, makes love with the light out.'

'Well, we make love with the lights out, that's only because I don't like seeing him enjoy himself.'

They were laughing when Brad walks over with Stevie's drink.

'What's the joke?'

'He was just saying he was with this girl once who was so ugly he kept the light off. Right, Stevie, you should contact Lucy. I mean now! No time like the present.'

'The thing is, I've lost my confidence.'

'I can imagine how that is. Not speaking to adults all day, you would get like that.'

'He spends all day with me,' Brad corrected his wife.

'Yes I know Brad, that's what I mean.'

'Oh ha ha, is it take the rip out of Brad night?'

'Stevie, message Lucy. She seems nice. Tell her everything about yourself then, when you meet, you don't have to worry about the elephant in the room.'

'Oh, he told you about Grace, then.'

'That was the fat one?'

'Fat!'

'Was she really fat? Obese.'

'Oh she was a beast all right. But you are right, tell her about my previous partners and the heart ache they left me with.'

'Oh please mate, pass me a hankie.'

'Funny, Brad. You know I have had more sense spoken to me in the last 5 minutes with Alice than a working life with you.'

Stevie takes his phone back and swiped something and put it past.

'So, what have you been talking about?'

'Brad, we were just surprised that with all your experience with women that you struggled in your role as Love Guru.'

'Ha bloody ha.'

Stevie's pinging phone interrupted. He took it out, apologising for using it on a night out.

'It's Lucy, she has got back to me right away. Is that a good sign?'

'No, mate, that's not good. Showing signs of desperation in my book.'

'Stevie, don't listen to him. What does she say?'

'Hi Stevie. I am Lucy, I am a 40 year old widow. My husband died 12 years ago. I have a teenage son who put me up to going on this Dating site. You are the first person to show an interest when I mention I am a single parent.'

'There you go. Desperate and with an ankle biter,' the Love Guru offered his unwarranted advice.

'Stevie, how do you know if Brad is talking crap? His lips are moving. You know this Lucy
sounds ideal. Write back and tell her you have been single for 3 months and are looking for a long term relationship.'

'Yeah, sounds good. Brad, what is the name for a female Love Guru, because your wife has just got the job?'

Stevie's can't keep his hands still. In front of him he has a glass of cola. Brad has just polished off a curry was gulping down his second pint.

'You should have something to eat, mate, you can't go dating on an empty stomach.'

'No, I can't risk anything going wrong tonight. I think Lucy is the one. Which might seem dumb when I haven't even seen her in the flesh yet.'

'Well, remember Grace.'

'Oh I will never forget Grace. But Lucy says she does a lot of cycling. Could never imagine Grace on a bike. The thing is her husband died of cancer when her son was 2. He is 14 now and he thinks it's time she moved on. Her son has been encouraging her to start dating. This will be her first ever date since she got married and I feel the pressure is on me.'

Their conversation is interrupted by Stevie's belly rumbling.

'Heaven's sake man, have something to eat. Have something light, try their soup, it's home made and will line your stomach.'

'I think you are right, I better eat something.'

Stevie parks his car just past Lucy's house. Their date had

went perfectly as far as Stevie was concerned, he was feeling butterflies in his stomach, desperate for Lucy to have enjoyed the night too and wanting a repeat.

'I hope you enjoyed our date and will let me take you out again.'

'Yes, I have loved it. The only thing is eh.'

Stevie's stomach churned again, the butterflies from earlier had turned to grasshoppers and were hopping about like mad. This was the heave-ho. He was about to be dumped.

'The thing is I struggle to get babysitters but maybe we could meet up during the day instead of at night.'

Stevie blew out with relief. 'I thought you were going to give me the heave-ho.'

'No, you have been a gentleman all night. Not letting me pay for any of the drinks or go Dutch for the meals. I haven't been on a date for years, obviously and don't know what is expected, you know, sexually.'

'Oh, well a kiss or two is usually adequate on a first date.'

'That's if there isn't going to be a second date.' Lucy then placed a finger over Stevie's lips so that he knew he was to stop talking. She leaned over and kissed him. While kissing, she reached down and rubbed his groin. As the blood rushed to his cock she unzipped his trousers and stopped kissing and went down on him.

Stevie couldn't believe what was happening. He certainly wasn't expecting a blow job. He managed to relax long enough to start enjoying the experience.

The joy turned to despair. He couldn't help himself, he was going to fart. The rumbling in his stomach had turned to gas and the gas wanted out. No matter how hard he tried to squeeze his sphincter the inevitable happened, it slipped out. His only hope was that it would dissipate into the cloth of the chair.

Lucy stopped sucking. She lifted her head as she choked. Then, as she tried to lift her head clear, it banged off the bottom edge of the steering wheel sending it back down into his putrid groin area, just as he dropped another, more fierce fart. She gagged again only this time she was sick. The entire contents of her stomach, a two course meal and two vodkas and orange, cascaded out and over Stevie's groin and in his trousers.

Guts emptied, she pulled her head head up and hit the steering wheel again. Turning her head she managed to squeeze herself free then grabbed her bag and barged out of the car.

Before going off, Lucy turned back and stuck her head back in the car. 'You are fucking disgusting!' she shouted, then slammed the car do so hard the whole car shook.

'You are a dirty cow!' Stevie

Lucy must have heard through the closed window. She was heading off but turned back. 'You cannot talk, your balls are all sick!' she yelled from outside the car.

Stevie put his hands in his head. In a few seconds a dream date had turned into another nightmare. He shouted after her, trying to apologise but now was not the time to try and placate her.

He drew his trousers back together, tucked in his now deflated member and tried to get settled to drive off. It was then he realised the sick had run right into the crack of his arse.

Before leaving, he turned the car at the bottom of the road. Driving slowly past Lucy's house, he found it in darkness except for a light in what he assumed was the bathroom window. He thought he should be going in to apologise but now was definitely not the time to do it.

Stevie is sat at his desk, checking his emails. Brad walked in and sat down. They sit in silence while Brad just stares at his mate. Eventually he can't bear the silence.

'Well?'

'I don't want to talk about it.'

'I thought you would be gloating. How nice she was. How I had made you waste time with all those other women. Well, if it went wrong then at least it wasn't my fault this time. Take it up with your new Love Guru.'

'Oh no. It was your fault. You better eat. Settle your stomach with a little home made soup.'

'So what, you didn't shit yourself?'

'No. Maybe it would have been better if I had.'

'Well, come on, spill the beans.'

'Right, I will tell you but this goes nowhere. You tell no-one, not even Alice or I will kill you.'

'Right, tell no-one.'

'I mean it. I will kill you. And no laughing or I will make your death slow and painful.'

Brad nods. He had never heard his mate talk like that and was sure he meant it.

'So, the date was great. Went to the Italian on the High Street. Lovely meal, she had a few drinks. Conversation flowed, she is a lovely girl, not had it easy bringing up a kid on her own. She was so sympathetic about Karen coming out. So I drove her home. We kissed.'

'Sounds ideal. So, what went wrong? Did she text you after and dump you. I can imagine that happening.'

'Are you going to let me finish. She didn't text me or anything. She hasn't contacted me at all.'

'Have you contacted her? Maybe she is looking for your approval. If I was still your Love Guru I would say wait for her to contact first but I can see you really liked this one. You should contact her.'

'No!'

'What is it? What are you not telling me?'

'You will just laugh.'

'I am saying I won't but I probably will.'

'Then I am saying nothing.'

'Come on, you can't leave it at that. Now you said it was my fault, so what have I got to feel guilty about.'

'Right, she said it was a lovely evening and she wanted to pay me back for it. So she went down on me.'

'No. You lucky bastard. Blow job on the first date. So, what went wrong, she found out about your tiny cock?'

'No. No, much worse that that?'

'She found out you have no cock?'

'No. Worse. I farted.'

'When? During the blow job?'

'Mid-suck.'

'No!'

'It gets worse.'

'Did she bite it?'

'No. She gagged on it.'

'No way. Well your farts have done that to me in the past.'

'It gets worse. After that she was sick. Right there, over my bollocks.'

Brad titters then after a struggle bursts out in laughter. Stevie rages at Brad but eventually laughs too.

'I have had two showers now but I still think I have some in the cracks of my scrotum'

Stevie was looking at his computer screen but not seeing what was on it.

'Stevie!'

No response.

'Stevie!'

Still nothing.

'Stevie!!'

Stevie came out of his trance.'You didn't need to shout.'

'Yes I did. 3 times I shouted you. You have been like this for a week now. Your work is starting to suffer. Why don't you contact her?'

'How do you know that's why I am like this? And why does she not contact me?'

'Maybe she is a stubborn so and so too.'

'The thing I don't understand is why did she give me a blow job? Everything had been going great.'

'And then I went and spoiled it all by giving Stevie- a blow job,' Brad sang.

'It isn't funny. Why do you think she did it? Would you expect it? Sorry, you are the last person I should be asking that.

You would be expecting the Kama Sutra.'

'Maybe she likes the taste of spunk.'

'You are sick. You always take it too far.'

'You are right. That wasn't even funny. Okay I think it could be one of two things. Firstly you should remember she probably hadn't been on a date for years. So, she has asked a friend what she should do at the end of the date and her friend suggested not to have sex but a blow job could be okay. Or, she thought she liked you and wanted you to know how much.'

Stevie pondered it for a few minutes. 'You know, you could be right.'

'So.'

'So, if she gets in touch, I will see her again.'

'For God's sake man, you know how lovely she is, how easy to talk too, blah, blah, blah. Be the bigger person.'

Stevie just shook his head.

'You know something Steven, sometimes you can be a right fud.'

Lunchtime and Stevie was in the pub alone. Brad racked up 15 minutes later.

'Where were you, your pint will be flat?'

'Shooting arrows.'

'What?'

'Never mind. You will find out.'

'What are you up too?'

'Little arrows in your clothing, little arrows in your hair,' he sang gently.

Next day and the humdrum of the office continued with boring normalcy until Stevie's phone pinged with a text.

'I don't understand this. Thanks for the flowers and letter.' He looked at his mate.

'Stevie, what are you smiling at? What have you done?'

'Something you should have done ages ago.'

'Flowers?'

'A bouquet of roses.'

'How much?'

'£20 you owe me.'

'And the letter?'

'I will send you a copy.'

Stevie's computer pinged, he checked it then read out from the email that Brad had just sent him.

'Lucy, our date last week was the best night out I have had in years, except of course for the last bit. What happened happened. If I could turn back time until you kissed me goodnight then I would and everything would have been perfect. We would probably have seen each other several times by now. But what happened happened, I cannot change that. However, if we could put this behind us I think we would be great together.

When you smiled I could see a sadness behind your eyes. I want to take this sadness away and replace it with happiness. If you think the same get in touch.'

Stevie turned round with a little tear in his eye. 'That's beautiful man. Where did that come from?'

'From you. I have been hearing you talk about Lucy for so long now that I think I know her. I also know that's the way you feel about her.'

'Wait a minute, how did you know where she lived?'

'I am a computer geek. You have given me enough clues over the week, finding her was easy.'

'So, what do I say next?'

'Ask her out again. She will say yes.'

'Okay, here goes.' He sends a text.

Like expectant fathers, time seems to stand still as they wait for a ping. Two minutes later it goes.

'Oh yes. Result. Robin is having a sleep-over at a friends on Saturday. Come over at 7. Kiss. You did it, mate. Your idea worked a treat.'

'All thanks to the Love Guru.'

HARRY'S STORY

HARRY felt great. He had a great score going on the video game. Highest level he'd made it too on this new game when he was interrupted by a knock on the bedroom door. He paused the game and hoped mum would only be a minute. She was forever in titivating and moving his stuff about although she usually did it when he was out.

'Enter if you dare,' he announced. He turned and to his surprise it wasn't his mother but his father. He stood sheepishly in the doorway, as if waiting to be asked in.

Harold, in his son's mind, had always been like that. Not the type of person to push himself.

'What's up?'

His father edged himself into the room, as if he didn't want to be there or, more importantly, that mother couldn't hear the conversation.

'Your mum said it's about time we had a wee man to man chat.'

'What, the birds and bees? A bit late for that, dad, I am nearly 30. I know the stork delivers babies but I never found out who shags the stork. Is that what you are going to tell me?'

Harold sort of harrumphed, he didn't like that kind of

talk, before continuing. 'This isn't a time for crude humour. Anyway, that joke is as old as you. Obviously you are at the singular stage of the birds and bees. Hand relief we used to call it, that of course was before I married your mum.'

'Is this a talk about, me wanking?'

'Oh no, we have known you have been doing it for years. Mum says when she shakes your bedsheets the rooms like the inside of a snow-globe. No, well, the thing is you are, as you say, nearly 30 and still living here, with your parents.'

'You want me to move out?'

'Well, not right away, we are not throwing you out yet but we think it's about time you got a girl and settled down in your own place.'

'So move out.'

'Well, that should be your ultimate aim. And also, your mother wants a craft room. So, the sooner you stop playing those silly games and get on Dating Websites, or whatever you do nowadays, the better.'

'Mother's idea?'

'No, we both agreed.'

'After mum decided. Well, can I at least finish this game first,' Harry said sarcastically as his father retreated from the room.

Next morning, Harry couldn't wait to tell his sister about the fatherly chat he had to listen to the night before. He worked with his sister at her hair and beauty salon. Sally is attractive and well presented, as salon owners usually are. After all Sally's mission is- come in and you too could look glamorous like me.

Harry checked the bookings for the day while Sal prepared her combs, scissors and the other tools of her trade.

'Did you know dad had a talk with me last night?'

'Yes, mum put it on Facebook. About, you know.'

'About me getting a girlfriend and moving out. No time limit but basically asap.'

'Oh, I thought it was about the eh, hand relief.'

'Mum plastered me wanking all over the Internet?'

'Well, she says you've been plastering the sheets for years.'

'So, who knows about it? What Facebook page is it on?'

'She did try and put in on to be private but you know mum and technology. So, it's just on the Salon's page.'

'Just the Salon's page! Just the Salon's page! So, what, all the customers know.'

'Not them all. Just the ones that are on Facebook.'

'Jesus, I think she must be trying to embarrass me out. You see the talk dad gave me was about moving out so that mum could have a Craft room. Mum wants a Craft room, I have to get out. Oh, and I have to get a girlfriend first, according to them. Obviously not wanting me to move into a flat and spend all my spare time wanking. Oh, the shame that would bring to the family.'

'Well, let's face it. Nearly 30, your mum does everything for you, cooks, cleans, irons your clothes.'

'Right, okay. Whose side are you on? Sorry, sis, maybe she has a point.'

'So, you are looking for a girlfriend. Do you want me to introduce you to any of my friends?'

'No, I know your friends, they are all as nutty as a handbag full of frogs.'

'Speaking of frogs, the dating agency my friends use is called Kissing Frogs. They all say it's very good. It's also in your price range, it's free.'

'Canny be that good if it's free.'

'That obviously depends if it's girls you are after.'

'What? Why would it not be? Do you think I bat for the other side? Drop anchor in pooh bay. Has my wrist ever been limp?'

'Well, there are a few things that pointed that way.'

'Like, for instance.'

'You work in a Ladies Hairdressers.'

'I wasn't working and you offered me a job. I wasn't sure at first but after a while I began to like it. Now, I can honestly say I love it and I love working with my big sister.'

'Secondly you have never had a girlfriend.'

'Yes I have. I just wouldn't let on to you lot or mum would be off getting a mother of the bride get up. Bring somebody to the house, next thing mums got a subscription for Bride magazine.'

'Come on, mum isn't that bad. No, you are right, she is. So, could you not afford to get a flat on your own?'

'On the money you pay me?'

'Well, I can't pay you any more.'

'I know sis, you see me alright.'

The bell sounds to herald a customer. A blond, 50 something walks in. She is all tanned and caked with make-up. She is also mutton dressed as lamb. Women her age shouldn't wear leather trousers, so unforgiving with a figure that has lived a life. She also has a preference for push-up bra's but not much too push up.

'Hi Tracey, punctual as ever.'

'Oh, I always come on time. Ask my husband if you want,' her tongue firmly in cheek.

Forty minutes later and Sally has worked her magic. She walked over to Harry in, what must have been in her mind, a seductive manner. To him, though, she looked like some-one who had previously had a stroke or other medical trauma.

'Looking beautiful again, Tracey.'

'Takes a bit more work than it used to but worth the effort, don't you think?'

'Oh, yes. And if you've got it, flaunt it.'

'I hope you don't think about me when you are, you know, fiddling. Or do you?'

'No. What are you talking about?' Although he asked, he knew exactly what she was on about.

'Well, we know about your wee hobby.'

'What? Oh, that thing on Facebook. My mum was at the wind-up. She just wants me to move out and thinks embarrassing me will help give me a push to go.'

'Oh, well, I have a spare room, I wouldn't mind a lodger My hubby works away from home a lot and it would be good to have a man in the house, I would sleep easier. Of course, you wouldn't need to be doing any of that fiddling with yourself then.'

'Right, I will keep it in mind.'

Tracey pays by switch then leaves but not before turning and blowing Harry a kiss at the front door.

Sally walked over from her next customer. 'What was Tracey offering?' she whispered.

'Room and board with free banging. She is looking for a lodger with a todger.'

'Something to think about,' she said with a wink.

Harry shuddered at the thought. 'If I tell you I am moving in with her, kill me because I have obviously lost my marbles.'

Harry spends lunchtime in the back shop. Normally he will surf the web for hints and tips to improve his gameplay. Today, he has other things to search for.

'Sally, do you think this frog thing is any good?'

'So the girls say. Easy too, a few simple questions and you are away.'

'Right, lets see.'

Harry's fingers move across the laptop keys with great dexterity.

'Right, Harry Malone. Food Indian, drink Lager. Film Borat, fucking legend. Actor Jason batter everyone Stratham. TV show The Office, Colour yellow. Finally job. What do you think for my job, Administration Assistant?'

'I would prefer tea boy, sweeper upper and general dogsbody.'

'There isn't enough room for all that. Anyway, when you put it like that, maybe I should be getting paid more.'

'Maybe you should but I am afraid you have 2 chances of getting more.'

'Yes sis, none and fuck all. Right, Office Administrator, that will do. Next, singer Rihanna. Song, Don't stop the music.

That's a song, isn't it sis.'

Harry sings 'Don't stop the music,' and his sister joins in. They sing a couple of lines then run out of words.

'Last question, favourite season, summer. That's it, send. Come to daddy, girls.'

'What if your only reply is from Tracey?'

'In your words, two chances.'

Things are quiet in the Salon so Harry spends the time sitting behind the counter, surfing.

Sally is giving Grace, an elderly customer, a blue rinse.

'Harry is on the Internet, trying to get a girl.'

'What, with all the talent that comes in here?' Grace cajoles.

Sally starts to laugh then realises Grace was serious. Meanwhile, Harry, who can hear them talk whispers to himself-'If there were any that didn't pish themselves maybe I might.' Most of their clientele were retired.

'Think he is going on a date tonight but he won't tell me anything about it. Thinks I will tell mum.'

Harry laughs sarcastically, loud enough for them to hear him.

Grace looks in his direction. 'Well, maybe it will stop him wanking.'

Harry paces along the front of the sports bar. Gaby gets off the bus and walks towards him. She looks younger than he though. She said she was 22. Maybe she was after all. He was so used to the vintage clientele he saw everyday at work that it was hard to age young people.

'Gaby.'

'Harry.'

They cuddle. The heady aroma of perfume fills his nostrils. God, how good it would be to be with a woman again, although Gaby seemed more like a girl. In that moment he realised how wrong his priorities had been for too long. Maybe his parents were right, get a girl and get out.

Gaby was dressed in trendy jeans that had so many cuts she should have got them for half price. She was wearing a leather jacket and white t-shirt. She was slim and had very small breasts. Her elfin haircut made her look even younger.

In the bar, Gaby found a table while Harry got the drinks in. Gaby was drinking vodka and coke while Harry stuck to gin.

'Am I ready for this,' he said as he put the drinks down.

'Me too.'

'By the way, I have a confession to make. This is the first time I have been on a date for years.'

Gaby's eyes widened. 'Have you been inside? That would be so cool, dating a jailbird.'

'No. I just haven't been bothered, you know, with girls.'

Again she seemed surprised. 'Have you been trying being gay? I could be the reason you turned back to women.'

'No I've not been trying men. I've just been happy being on my own. Now, I think it's time for a bit of company.'

'Listen, don't worry. I've not been on a date for ages either. Not much of a drinker either, must have been thirsty.'

Her glass was empty before Harry had touched his drink.

Harry sipped his gin and studied his new beau. She looked young, much younger than the 22 years she said she was.

'So, you are 22 and you are a student.'

'Yes.'

'What are you studying?'

She paused then said, 'A bit of everything.'

'Oh, right. Are you at the college or Uni?'

'College,' she said, again after a pause.

The pausing between answers bothered Harry.

'Ready for another drink?'

'Yes.'

As he stood at the bar waiting for the next drinks, it was plain from the girl's body language that Gaby was ripe for the picking. However, it bothered him about her age and the fact he had no-where to take her. He was sure she was still staying at home too.

'Here's your drink. Where are you staying at the moment? I am still living at home.'

Gaby paused again. 'I live in a flat but it's my flatmate Jenny's turn to bring a fellow round. You know, we take turns. We can always go round the back of the club. It's always quiet round there.'

Before Harry could sip his new gin Gaby had half finished her drink.

'Would you like that? To go round the back of the pub,' she asked but was already starting to slur her words.

'Think you should go a bit slower with the firewater.'

'Firewater,' she laughed. 'This is like coke to me.'

'Try telling your eyes that, they are glazing over.'

'Oh, are you trying to get me drunk?'

'No, I think you are doing okay for yourself.'

'Right. Drink up and we will go round the back.'

'I think I will go out and call you a taxi.'

'You can call me anything you want, as long as you take me round the back.'

'Wait until I finish my drink.'

Outside and a nice, cooling breeze is blowing. The fresh air has an almost instant effect on Gaby making her even drunker. She reaches round and grabs Harry round the neck. She kisses him and he responds.

'Look, we shouldn't be doing this. Come on and I will put you in a cab.'

'No, I don't want to go in a cab. I want to go round the back. I will let you do me. Anyway, I don't have money for the cab fare. Come on round the back. Please.'

She grabs him and kisses him again. The nice perfume from earlier was replaced with alcoholic smelling breath that was coke with a salty tang.

'Your breath tastes salty. Have you been eating nuts or

something?'

'No, I was sick in the toilet before we came out. I feel better now.'

Suddenly Harry felt nauseous, he had been sticking his tongue in her mouth.

'Come here, so I can whisper something,' she says, 'Can I tell you something. I want you to do me. But I don't want to get pregnant so we need to do anal.'

Her whisper was louder than her normal voice thanks to the drink. Harry looked round to make sure nobody passing could hear.

'I've never done anal,' he whispered in her ear.

'Well, tonight's the night.'

'I think it's time you were home. Come on round to the taxi rank. It's okay, I will pay.'

'No, I don't want paid for the sex. You bought me drinks.'

'I don't want sex.'

'You think I am ugly?' She puts on a sad face that turns to pleading. 'Please have sex with me! I don't want to be a virgin any more. My friends aren't virgins. Come on, lets go round the back.'

'No, I just mean not tonight, not when you are drunk. Another night maybe. What about tomorrow?'

'Drunk? I am not drunk. I only had 2 drinks.'

'You had 4 and you drank them too quick. That's why you were sick.'

The peace was shattered by the screeching of a car's tyres as a car slid to an abrupt stop.

Harry looked up and saw a middle aged couple who were staring at them from a car parked at the curb.

'Mum! Hey, that's my mum.' Gaby waves over.

'Oh God.' Harry had a terrible, sinking feeling in his gut.

Gaby's father burst out of the car and powered towards them. It was strange to imagine this was his daughter. He was short, fat and had a mass of red hair and a face beneath that matched it.

'What are you doing with my daughter?' her father raged,

pointing a finger in Harry's face.

'Nothing,' Harry said, as he angled Gaby to be between her and her father who was one angry bunny.

Harry was grabbed by the shirt by the raging parent.

'Do you know she is only 16. Look at her, she's drunk. What kind of sick fuck are you, getting a young girl drunk?'

'What 16? She told me she was 22.'

'Don't dad. Can you not leave us? We were just going round the back of the club. We were going to do anal.'

'What? You dirty bastard!'

Harry moved away only to me met by an unstoppable object. He managed to half turn his head to find his escape blocked by Gaby's mother, a squat fat woman who would probably be taller lying down and was well fitted to being a human barricade. He turned back, raising his hands to try to reason with the father only to me met by a fist to the face.

He felt a taste of blood in his mouth then the next thing he new he was eating the pavement.

Harry walked slowly into the salon next morning. He thought of phoning in sick but his mother did the big house clean on a Wednesday, so he would be better off at work. He would get no peace there.

'Don't remember you asking for a half-day.'

'Ha ha. Anyway, I am not that late. And, could you please stop the shouting.'

'I am not shouting. Oh, right, rough are you? Serves you right, drinking on a week night. You should know better than to drink when you have work the next morning. So, what's the sunglasses for? Your new cool image?'

'I had a drink but that's not the problem. The girl I was out with was supposed to be 22 but turned out to be only 16. Her father turned up and decked me. That's the reason for the shades.'

'Here, let me see.'

Sally left her customer and walked over to see the damage.

'Boy oh, that's a shiner. Caught your lip as well. If that was one punch, he must have a hand like a shovel.'

'He did. Then his wife kicked me in the knackers when I was down.'

'So, why did you not phone the Police?'

'Oh right, that would look good. Plying a 16 year old with vodka and coke. What was my little game eh?'

The customer tries to look up from under the dryer. 'Vinegar and brown paper, that's what to put on it.'

'What?' Harry asked.

'Vinegar and brown paper for a black eye.'

'That's for a broken crown and my name isn't Jack.'

'Sally, that's what you use, isn't it Sally?'

'Yes, Mrs.Burns. I have some in the back room, won't be minute.

They went through to the back room.

'Why did you not phone in sick?'

'Wednesday is deep clean day. It would be quieter with my head beneath one of your dryers.
You know she only stops cleaning for a family death or a Royal Wedding. As if that wasn't bad enough, mum started on at breakfast about how she was going to get dad to decorate her Craft room. God, she was doing my head in.'

'So, why did your date's father hit you?'

'Well, she was only 16. Told me she was 22. She had 4 vodkas that she drank like water and she was drunk. Then she wanted me to take her out the back and, well, take her up the bum.'

'You didn't!'

'No. I was trying to get her in a taxi when her parents drew up in their car. Honest, all we did was kiss but we never did anything else.'

'So, are you going to see her again?' Sally asked, laughing.

'Are you kidding? No, am oot, as they say on Dragon's

Den.'

Harry sat at the Sports Bar nursing a pint. The front door opens and a stunning blonde walks in. All the male heads turn at this woman who is well over six foot. She was wearing a short skirt that enhances the length of her legs and barely hid her knickers.

As she walks towards the bar, Harry, who had also been staring, realised it was Stephanie, his date. She looked good in her picture but in the flesh she was Page 3 stuff. He got off his stool, waiting to welcome her.

'Stephanie?'

'Oh.'

'Oh what?'

'Well, you are a lot shorted than your internet picture.'

'By the same token, you are a lot bigger than yours.'

With that, Stephanie turns and walks out.

Harry turns to the barman who looks as bemused as him. 'Not as big as my picture?'

The barman laughed but also looked over Harry's shoulder to watch the dolly bird leave.

'She's got some arse on her,' he said but Harry never noticed.

'Can you believe that? A week of talking on the Net and not a mention that she is a human fucking giraffe. Then she blames me for being a too fucking small. Fucking cow!'

'So what is she, a giraffe or a cow?'

'Both, that's why she is so fucking big. Anyway, it wouldn't have lasted. Eventually I would have had to jack it in.'

Harry decided the Sports Bar was giving him bad karma in the dating game. Luckily a new Greek restaurant had opened recently. Barbara, his next possible concubine, had said she loved foreign food. Harry booked the table and they agreed to meet inside.

After the previous two disasters, Harry was more cautious. Looking back it might seem furtive but instead of being in the restaurant waiting, he watched from across the road.

Barbara, or the person who he thought matched her description, arrived dead on time.
From the other side of the road she seemed, well, okay. Taking a deep breath he marched across to his date fate.

The waiter showed Harry to his table where Barbara was already seated.

'Sorry I'm a bit late, the taxi was held up,' Harry opened with.

'Oh, you are not late at all, I am early.'

'Lets order drinks. Do we just start with wine?'

The waiter was signalled and the menu's brought over.

'I don't usually do wine, could you order?'

'Me neither. Tell you what, get the waiter to choose for us.'

'Sure, lets make it one of those nights eh, anything goes.'

Barbara studies the menu and is very quiet. Harry starts to worry that he is not her type and she is thinking of an excuse to leave.

Looking over his own menu so he can study her, he sees she is nearer 40 than 30. She had said she was 30 plus but the plus looked as if it could have been 15 or 20 more years. Still, she seemed nice. She wore minimum make-up but he preferred that to women with it trowelled on. The woman for him? Maybe not but if he got a bit of action that would be a result. Good to get back on the old hobby horse.

'Is there something wrong?'

'It's very expensive.'

'Oh, don't worry, I will pay.'

'Gosh, no. We have to go Dutch.'

'Dutch, I thought we were going Greek.'

'I meant half each.'

'I know, just my little joke.'

Harry smiled but Barbara didn't. Oh-oh, he thought, sense of humour bypass. This could be a long, dull night.

The food was good, Harry's first go at Greek but it was all

fresh and tasty. The date however was neither fresh nor tasty. Barbara wouldn't open up about herself and went quiet for a short while after he said he worked at a Ladies Beauty Salon. Even the offer of a discount didn't break a smile.

While they were waiting for their coffees, Barbara excused herself and nipped to the Ladies.

Twenty minutes later, she hadn't returned. The waiter had been hovering by his table, probably desperate to get the table cleared and get home.

'Excuse me,' Harry asked the waiter, 'My friend went to the toilet a while ago. Could somebody check that she is okay.'

The waiter went to the bar and asked a female worker to check the Ladies. She returned and put her arms out. She had gone. Gone. Disappeared. Given him the elbow without even a goodnight kiss. Harry couldn't believe it, dumped again. Although this time she had enjoyed a slap up meal on him.

After paying the bill, Harry walked down to the bus stop. Waiting for the bus, he tried contacting his date. Barbara's number came back unattainable. Fucking bitch.

Across the road there was a woman waiting for the bus going the other direction. For a moment Harry thought it looked like Barbara but this woman was blonde and wearing trousers, a different coloured jacket and had a headscarf on her head. Mind you, her handbag was a huge thing. Anyway, it was dark, he couldn't be sure. He stared over then shouted- 'Barbara!' The woman put her head down. It was her. What a dolt he had been. She had obviously gone to the toilet, changed and put a wig on and given him the dizzy. Sneaked away but was now thwarted as the bus was late.

Harry was ready to cross the road when the bus arrived to whisk Barbara out of his life. The traffic on his side of the road thwarted his progress. At the first break he was across the road. Barbara was on the bus by then and sat at up the back on the seats nearest Harry.

Harry ran up to the back of the bus. He rapped on the window. Barbara clearly heard him but turned away.

'Barbara! Barbara!'Harry shouted. 'Bet your name isn't even Barbara. Hope you get food poisoning, you sneaky bitch!' he roared at her.

The bus drove off with Harry watching as it left. Barbara, if that was even her name, never even turned her head towards him.

Harry was getting no shortage of interest from the dating app. With three failed dates, he decided to changing tack. Harry decided to have a pre-date coffee with his next date. Although there were plenty of willing suitors. The problem was they all seemed to be nutters. He had the feeling his next choice, Arlene would be different.

Arlene arrives and is quite tall but not giraffe-like. She was pretty with long black hair down past her shoulders. It took him a little while to realise she wasn't wearing any make-up at all but she was still pretty. Her dress sense was a bit plain Jane but that didn't bother him either.

They both ordered Mocha's and declined any food. Of the dates he had been on so far, Arlene was by far the easiest to talk too. They were about the same age. She was a dental hygienist, when she told Harry he thought you can floss me anytime but decided not to try humour at this early stage. The golden nugget with this girl, she had her own flat. Result. If only he could get her round there.

Coffees drained, Harry thought it best to make his move.

'Fancy going for a burger?'

'A burger?'

'Yes. Monday night special at the Crown Inn is burger and beer for £6.'

Suddenly Arlene was on her feet and turned on Harry. 'You eat meat?'

'Yes. I like a good steak.'

'I'm a Vegan. You Cow murderer! Oh, you might not do the slaughtering yourself but you provide the mechanism for its death.'

She got up and every head in the busy cafe turned to see what the fuss was about.

'You have animals blood on your hands!' she said, pointing an accusing finger.

That said, she stormed out of the coffee shop and out of Harry's life. What he couldn't fathom was if being a Vegan was such a big issue for her, why wait until they are on the date to drop the bombshell. He sat drinking his coffee with everyone in the coffee shop staring at him. Still, he enjoyed the burger and beer he had before going home.

Next morning Harry was sitting at the salon's desk. Sally walked over and sat next to him.

'Well, it's been a fortnight now, how's the Dating going?'

Harry gave her a look but said nothing.

'Look, this is between us. No mum, no Facebook.'

'No Ethan.'

'No, I won't tell my husband either.'

'Yes you will, you tell him everything.'

'Well, that's what marriage is all about. For once though I will keep it to my self.'

'Thanks but don't expect an engagement soon. In fact, pardon my French, but it's been an absolute fucking disaster. First date you know her father turns up and clocks me. Then I get a dumb fuck who turns up, says I look smaller than my profile picture and walks out. Third one we go Greek. She eats her meal then sneaks out of the restaurant. So, I take a new tack. Meet in a coffee shop. Everything is going fine so I suggest going for a burger. Oh, that's when she tells me she is a vegan. I mean, it's not as if we hadn't been texting for days. You know, if it's really important to you, tell people.'

'No luck at all then. What about my friend Mary?'

'Scary Mary? No, I think I would take up Tracey's offer before going out with Mary.'

'Well you are in luck, Tracey is back in today.'

'Look, things have been bad but they are not that bad yet.

Hey, is Mary still making her own clothes?'

'No. She has gone upmarket now, gets them from charity shops.'

'God, I still have nightmares about the bikini she crocheted and wore when she was on holiday with us. Remember when it got wet and sagged. I saw things a 12 year old should never see.'

'So, will I tell Tracey you are still mulling her offer over? After all, there's plenty a good tune played on an old fiddle.'

'Maybe so but she is getting nowhere near my bow. You have always said there is somebody for everybody, I just have to kiss a few more frogs. Christ, it would be good to even get to the kissing stage.'

'Tell you what, show me your Dating App and I will help you choose your next date.'

Harry opens the Kissing Frogs app at his page. Sally surveys the girls looking for men.

'What about Sophie? Seems like a nice girl.'

'Suppose she is all right looking.'

'Oh, I forget you were a Page 7 model.'

'Okay, I will swipe it but on your head be it.'

They are interrupted by the dinging of the door alarm. Tracey has entered and trailing behind her a gent in his 50's. They are dressed in matching sports gear looking like they had just done a photo-shoot for a Saga sports day.

The old guy walks over to the desk while Tracey makes herself comfortable in Sally's chair.

'Are you Harry? I am Terry, Tracey's husband.'

'Pleased to meet you.'

'Tracey tells me you are looking for a room.'

'Yes but I am really looking for a flat. Anyway I am not that desperate yet that I would move in with somebody. Not that I would need to be desperate to move in with you. It's just I would prefer a place of my own.'

'Oh I understand, bit of peace for your, you know, relief.'

Harry turns to see Tracey smiling at him. She must have

told him everything and now the bloke must think he is constantly playing with himself.

'Well, the thing is, as you may know I work away from home a lot. It would give me peace of mind to know there was a man in the house. Tracey might seem to be a strong woman but she worries when she is in the house alone.'

'Oh, I understand, but as I said, I am not that desperate yet.'

'That's not what Tracey says. Seems that your mother puts it different on Facebook.'

'She is an awfy joker, my mum.'

As he leaves he tells Tracey he would get her on his way back from the gym.

When Tracey's transformation is complete, she walks over to the desk. Sports gear is not forgiving. With Lycra type clothes, every lump and bump is on show. Harry's eyes were drawn to the crotch area. Christ, what did she have down there? Then he felt embarrassed, maybe it was medical, a prolapse or something although it looked, by the unsightly bulge, as if half of her guts had dropped out.

'Well, ready to take up my offer?'

'Oh, no. The dating is going great.'

'So, no wanking then?'

'No. All my needs catered for.'

'Good. But remember my offer still stands.'

'I will keep it in mind.'

As she left, Sally walked over.

'What's wrong with you? Looks like you saw a ghost?'

'Worse. I saw Tracey in Lycra. I think it was pushing her insides out. Yeurgh!'

Harry gets a coffee from the counter. He is taking a chance meeting Sophie in the same coffee shop as the last time but it can't be as bad. As he scans the room he doesn't recognise anybody from the previous incident.

Sophie is already seated and is drinking bottled water.

She is prettier in real life than she was on her profile picture. Harry would wangle that into the conversation if he could. She wasn't fat, more muscly, obviously works out. She had just turned 30 and her parents had bought her a flat near the harbour. He decided not to tell her his parents were set to get him evicted for his 30th.

Harry got himself a coffee and joined her.

'So,' Sophie asked, 'Do you work out much?'

Harry was surprised that this was her opening gambit, she hadn't mentioned it on her profile.

'What the gym like? Oh sure, used to be a member at the one in the hotel but they put the prices up so much. So I left there meaning to go to another gym but other things took over and I just stopped going.'

'Oh, you should always make time for a work out. Big strong guy like yourself.'

Harry felt himself redden a bit.

'You are right, I should get back into it.'

'So, how do you fancy a gym date night?'

'A what?'

'A gym date night. It's the latest craze. You work out then go and make out.'

'Sounds great,' Harry said trying to sound as if he meant it but deep down he felt a huge regret, knowing how unfit he was.

'What about Friday?'

'This Friday? Well, I don't have a membership anywhere,' he said, looking for a get out.

'It's okay, my gym allows you to take a friend along, you know a sort of try before you buy.'

'Okay then, Friday it is.' What he actually meant was- oh Holy fuck.

Sophie was warming up gently. She had a stunning body. Harry looked away. He couldn't look in case he got turned on and his shorts, that he hadn't worn for ages, were not very forgiving.

Any sign of a bulge would show instantly.

'Treadmill first then,' Sophie says.

Harry gets on the machine next to hers. They start slow but get a bit faster. Harry manages to keep pace with her but his legs are burning before they stop.

'How are you on a bike?' she asks.

'Better going down hill,' he joked.

This time he goes at a slower pace than her. He had to, there was little left in the tank.

By the time they finish, Harry is drenched, Sophie has a little sweat on her brow.

'Grab some water then they will do some weights.'

As Harry lifted his hand tremble a bit which worried him as he hadn't even started on the weights.

The shower room came as a relief. Every bit of him ached.

Having stripped off he stood beneath the shower and let it run over his battered body. He was joined by another guy who had been using the treadmill after them.

'You with Sophie then?'

'Not actually with her. It's just our first date. She seems to be a nice girl.'

'Oh yes, really nice. Cracking body and she knows how to use it.'

'Oh yes, she is well put together.'

'A word of warning, my mate went out with her, wore him out after 3 weeks. Bloody nympho.'

'Obviously not got the stamina I have' he joked.

Monday morning and Harry walks into the salon, gingerly, a shadow of his normally chipper self.

Sally bursts out laughing. 'What happened to you?'

'Sophie happened to me.'

'What, did she beat you up?'

'No. We went on a gym date then back to hers. A guy in the showers warned me about her but it still didn't prepare me for what I got.'

'What?'

'Well, we were hardly in her flat door and she was pulling the clothes off me. Straight to bed we went. I went on top then she went on top then she did this reverse cowgirl thing. Don't know what other positions we did after that. God, there were positions I hadn't even seen on porn channels.'

'Do you think you should be telling me this?'

'I have got to tell somebody, salve my conscience or something like that. So we fall asleep,
then some time in the early hours I woke up to find her on top of me again. God knows how she did it. So I just lay there and let her get on with it.'

'In the morning we have cereal, in bed, then we start all over again. Good job I had Saturday morning off, although that might have saved me.'

'So, why did you stop?'

'Sunday morning she nipped out for bacon and eggs for breakfast and I sneaked away and got home. Straight in to bed I was, lay there until this morning recovering. God, her last boyfriend lasted 3 weeks. I only managed 2 days, so fair play to the guy.'

'Not tempted to go back and see her again?'

'Not unless I do a lot of marathon training first.'

'So, that's another one down. Want help to find your next eh challenge?'

'You bet. I have come this far, I ain't giving up now. We will check the girls out at lunch time.'

Harry and Sally are on the sofa in the Salon's back room studying Harry's tablet. Sally knew the next pick was important and she also wanted the best for her wee brother.

'Mavis?'

'Are people our age called Mavis? Well, she is blonde, that's a tick.'

'She might not be a natural blonde.'

'What, do you mean like an aeroplane blonde?'

Sally looked at him, not getting it.

'She will still have the black box.'

'I thought you were taking this seriously.'

'Okay, favourite film Bridesmaids.'

'I liked that film.'

'Favourite colour- bridal white. Seems too keen for a wedding. Next.'

'Christina.'

'Ginger.'

'Now Harry, not P.C.. Nowadays we call them strawberry blonde.'

'She might be strawberry blonde but she will have ginger pubes. And I do not want wee ginger babies.'

'First, you don't want a wedding soon, now you are talking about babies.'

'Well, accidents happen and I don't want a wee ginger accident. And strawberry blondes as you call them are renown for their fiery temper, that's the last thing I need.'

'Martina?'

Harry read her profile. 'She is not the type I would go for. Anyway, she is too nice looking.'

'Too nice looking? Where's the Malone fighting spirit, aim high.'

'I didn't know we had a fighting spirit. In fact, I didn't think we had any spirit.'

'She's my top pick.'

'Well, you go out with her. Sorry, didn't mean that. I am really glad of your help. Right, I will try Martina. You are sure she will want to go out with me.'

'Of course you will, you are a Malone.'

'As long as she doesn't know mum.'

Harry paces up and down the front of the Sports Bar like an expectant father. The butterflies in his stomach were having a rave. Last time he felt like this when he took Eva Fenton round the back of the Assembly Hall at the 3rd year disco. Why he was like this he didn't know, he hadn't been like it on any of the other dates.

A taxi drew up and he held his breath. Martina got out and smiled over at him. In that instant he fell in love. Or at least in lust. He drank her in. She was same height as him although she was wearing heels. Long black hair, nicely made up. She wasn't slim nor was she fat, Harry liked that. Stick thin girls, modelly types weren't his bag.

When they came together they air-kissed, both sides.

'That was lucky, usually when I try that I end up head-butting,' Harry said.

'Sorry, but if you head-butted me I would do it back to you.'

'In a nice way I hope.'

'Never mind that, lets get a drink. My mouth's like as dry as a Nun's twat.'

Harry burst out laughing. That was a new one to him but coming from a girl was even funnier.

If Carlsberg invented dates, Harry thought this would be close. Everything was going great. Martina was funny, liked Harry's corny jokes and told a good story herself. Over the night they had several drinks but neither was drunk.

Martina looked into Harry's eyes.

'So, are we going back to your place?'

Harry swallowed hard. This was where the date went Pete Tong.

'The thing is, I still live with my parents. If I took you back, even for a coffee, mum would be on-line, ordering a mother of the groom outfit. That's why I am dating. Mum wants a craft room and she wants me out.'

Martina started laughing. Serious laughing. Harry thought the joke was on him so didn't join in. Date over, he thought.

Martina took an age to compose herself.

'Sorry, I couldn't help it. You see, I am still living my parents. My dad wants me out because he wants a bar with a pool table in my room. So I suppose we are sort of soul mates.'

Harry could now afford to laugh.

'Is there nowhere else we could go? You not got any mates who would let you, you know, borrow a room for a few hours?'

'Sorry, I am Harry no mates at the moment. All my mates are married or coupled up. Wait, there is one place. Not for tonight though, I don't have the keys with me.'

'Where?'

'My sister's hair salon.'

'Oh, are you a stylist? I could do with a trim.'

'No, I am just a receptionist but I could get you a discount. Tell you what, what about Saturday night. Go for a curry, a few drinks then I will get the spare keys sis keeps at our place. Nip down to the salon for a bit of fun.'

Martina lifted her glass in a toast.

'To Saturday night and fun.'

'Saturday night, can't wait.'

Harry opens the salon as quietly as he could in his inebriated state. All the time shooshing Martina who had developed a fit of the giggles.

'We can only put the back lights on, don't want neighbours calling the Police.'

They staggered through to the back room and closed the door before putting the light on.

Sally and Ethan are curled up on the sofa watching TV. Ethan's phone pings.

'Oh my God, it's an alert from the salon.'

'Quick, phone the Police.'

'Hold on, wait until I see.'

Ethan flicks through the phone and an image appears. 'The horny sod.'

'What? Who?'

Sally leans over and shares the view.

'Oh, no. I forgot to tell Harry about the CCTV and alert system.'

'Well, that was the weekend he was on holiday, wasn't it?'

'Sure. Oh, I don't think I want to watch any more.'

'Jees, he's really going for it. Nice action.'

'Do you think I should phone him?' Sally asked.

'No, I think we should just switch off and leave him too it.'

'Tell you what, I won't be sitting on that sofa again.'

'Hold on, that was the sofa we had in the bedsit years ago. It saw plenty of action then.'

'But that was just us.'

In the salon, Harry and Martina are kissing post-coitus. For the first time in his life Harry felt he was in love, he only hoped Martina felt the same.

'I need to freshen up. Where are my knickers?'

They search the sofa but found them on the floor where they had landed. Underwear found, she went off to the toilet.

Harry couldn't get the grin off his face. Martina was great, the sex was great. The curry had been great. Suddenly a gurgling in his stomach told him it might have been nice going down but might want to come back out soon. Very soon. The gurgling turned to spasms. The spasms started coming quicker and one thing was certain, if Martina didn't come out quickly, he would shit on the floor..

Martina emerged smiling from the toilet. 'That's better. We could go again when you are up to it.'

'You will need to excuse me, I need to use the toilet,' Harry said as he walked past, holding his stomach and clenching his bum cheeks to avoid disaster. 'You sit on the sofa, I will try and not be long.'

Harry made it to the pan before the returning curry erupted from him with great volume, smell and heat. The relief though was palpable. After cleaning himself he relaxed before returning to see his new girl.

Harry woke with a start. He must have fallen asleep on

the toilet pan. He struggled to find his phone. To his relief he'd only dozed for about 15 minutes. After splashing water on his face, he was ready to continue his wonderful date.

Returning to the back room, Martina wasn't there. Looked like she had left him.

He hurried through to find the salon in darkness but Martina was there. Sitting on Sally's chair with her head under a hair-dryer. Harry flicked a switch to put the mirror light on only to discover smoke coming from under the dryer.

'For fucks sake, Martina, your hairs on fire!'

He rushed round and switched it off. He pulled the dryer off slowly and found her beautiful face topped with a mass of burnt, bedraggled and smoking hair. He then grabbed a towel, damped it in the sink and put it on her head. After a few minutes he lifts the towel, slowly and carefully.

'Is it bad?'

'Oh, it's bad.'

She started crying. 'My lovely hair!'

'It's not all bad, you look a bit like a TV star now.'

She stopped sobbing long enough to ask who.

'Ken Dodd.'

She started crying again. 'It's ruined. Ruined. My lovely hair.'

Harry stood away from the mirror so Martina could see her new style. It was flattened down and singed at the ends. She cried all the louder.

Harry leaned in and cuddled her.

'It will be all right. Wash and style it in the morning and it will be fine. Come on, we better get out of her before somebody sees us or hears you crying. I will get us a taxi.'

Outside, the couple cuddled and kissed, all the time Harry re-assured her that her hair would be fine in the morning. He only wished he believed it himself. By the time the taxi appeared though, Martina had calmed down. She thought it would be all right in the morning after a wash as Harry had promised.

Sunday morning, day of rest. Harry is in his wank chariot, sound to the World. The peace shattered by a banging on the front door.

'Harry!' his mums yells from the hallway. 'Harry!' seemed to echo up the stairs and round his head. He sat up in bed only to find in his drunken reverie he hadn't taken off any of his clothes. Or his shoes from the previous evening although he was tucked up soundly beneath the covers. In a panic, he rushed over to the window. A strange car was parked at the front gate and raised voices were coming from the outside the front door. Martina, he thought, it must be. What was she doing here? Oh no -her ruined hair. Still, nothing for it than to face the music, sounded as if somebody was getting angrier and angrier as the voices were getting louder.

As Harry gets to the bottom of the stairs, the welcoming party consisting of his mother and father, Martina and a middle aged man who must have been Martina's dad.

Martina is looking sheepish and wearing a woollen hat. Her father pulled the hat off to show a bedraggled mess that had once been a lovely head of hair.

Before he could speak, Harry clutched his stomach. 'Hold on, toilet,' he said and rushed past to the downstairs toilet. On the pan the last of the curry's revenge escaped painfully.

Between grunts, Harry managed to get his phone out. He dialled his sister. It seemed to ring for ages. 'Come on, come on, Sis, pick up.'

'Hello.'

'Sally, this is an emergency!'

'You haven't cut your hair again when you were drunk.'

'No, no. Worse that that. Much worse than that. This is life or death. My life or death.'

'Seriously.'

'Yes. Seriously. Martina is here and her hair is a mess. Her father is with her and he's build like a brick shit -house. Boy is he angry and he wants to take it out on my hide.'

'So, what happened?'

'Martina decided to stick her head below a hair dryer and it's all singed.'

'One of my dryers!'

'Yes but the dryer's okay, it's just her hair that's fucked.'

'How did she manage to use my dryer?'

'That's not important right now, this is an emergency!' he pleaded.

'Right, I will meet you at the salon in 15 minutes. Where are you just now?'

'At home. In the toilet. Oh no, severe ring sting.'

'Okay, enough, more than your sister needs to know. See you soon.'

Harry emerged from the toilet to find everybody talking at the same time, voices getting louder and louder, accusation and counter accusation flying between each side.

Martina's father, Jimmy, again pulled the hat from Martina's head. 'Look at the mess of this, stylist!'

Harry looked at Martina who cast her eyes downward.

'It's not that bad.' Not the best choice of words, talk about putting petrol on a fire to try to douse the flames.

'It's not that bad! Not that fucking bad! I will take a blow-torch to your hair and we will see how bad that is! You have ruined her lovely hair! God knows what you were playing at last night, you must be some kind of pervert.'

'Look, I have phoned my sister, she is a stylist. She will sort it. If we go to Sally's Salon she will meet us there and sort it.'

'Well, we are not paying!'

'No, I will sort it out.'

'This isn't the end of it!' her father said angrily.

What followed for Harry was the worst car trip ever. He sat in the back, shouting directions while Jimmy continued to rant and rave about the mess of his little darling's hair. Martina meanwhile sat in the front sobbing. There was palpable relief for him when they drew up and Sally was already in the salon. Harry and Martina got out the car, thankfully Jimmy stayed put.

Martina turned and quietly said, 'Thanks for not saying anything. I couldn't tell dad the truth.'

'It's okay, I've got broad shoulders. As long as he doesn't get violent.'

'His bark is worth than his bite.'

Sally was checking out her dryer and seemed happy it wasn't damaged. She sent Harry through to the back room. Martina settled into the stylist's chair and sat with her head down.

'So, what happened?'

'We were drunk and came back here after the pub. For some strange reason I decided my hair needed styled and put it under the dryer. Think I nodded off, next thing I know Harry was shouting and there was smoke and my hair ended up like this.'

'Had you washed it?'

Martina shook her head meekly.

'Been using hairspray?'

This time she nodded.

'You are lucky you are not bald.'

'Really!'

'Really. Anyway, it's mostly the tips, looks worse than it is.'

'Harry won't want to see me again after this.'

'Don't be silly. You are all he has talked about since your first date. He is really into you. That's the thing with the Malone's, we go for love at first sight. When I first saw Ethan I knew he was the one for me.'

'Is that your husband?'

'Yes, we've been married for five years.'

'Kids?'

'No but we are working on it.'

'I would like to get married.'

Sally finished her magic with a gentle spray of lacquer. She stood back to let the client see herself in the mirror.

Martina looked up and started crying.

Sally shouted Harry through and he arrived just as dad Jimmy appeared through the front door.

'What's wrong, why are you crying?'

'It's nothing dad, it's lovely.'

'It's just when I saw you crying again I thought the worst but I can't argue, she has done a great job.' He then turned to Sally. 'Can't say the same for your brother. Right, how much do I owe you?'

Harry intervened, 'No, I will settle up.'

'Least you can do after what you did to her. Come on love. I've not had my breakfast yet.'

Martina gave Harry a little wave as she was leaving.

'Thanks again Sally, love the new style. I will recommend you to all my friends.'

Brother and sister stood and watched as Martina and her dad drew away in the car.

'Shit, how am I supposed to get home?'

'Ethan will be back to pick me up in 10 minutes.'

'No, it's okay, I will walk. I need to clear my head anyway. Hopefully mum will have cooled down a bit. This is going to take some explaining. Anyway, thanks again sister, you are a lifesaver. So, do you think that's us over? You know, me and Martina.'

'What, you and Martina? No, all she did was talk about you. I think you two are made for each other. Don't know why, seems too nice for you.'

'Ha ha. Right, I will be off then. I will bring you something nice on Tuesday.'

'Tuesday? No, you will see me this afternoon. Did you forget, mums invited us over for one of her Sunday Roast specials.'

'Oh no, not again. The state my guts are in, it will end up down the pan.'

'That's not something your sister wants to think about.'

Harry's stomach gurgled as his mum brought the soup tureen through from the kitchen. The thought of food again was churning it up. He would have to have something, starving himself was making him feel weak. Told his mother one ladle full would do. One thing his mother could do was cook. Her home-made chicken broth was brill and should line his stomach a bit.

Ethan started talking. That was allowed, Ethan could do no wrong. If Harry spoke first the 'not at the dinner table' rule would have been rolled out.

'Did you hear the Pet shop down the road from the salon was broken into.'

Harold looked up from his soup. 'When was this then, Harry never said?'

'About a month ago.'

'Did they get much?'

'No, but it was the damage they did. Old Alec was hundreds out of pocket by the time he made good. He got CCTV put in so we followed suit. We've got fully functioning CCTV live in the salon now. Any trips and it sends an alert to my phone. '

Harry choked on his soup. When he stopped choking he managed to say-'When did you do this?'

'About 3 weekends ago. Remember the weekend you were on holiday.'

'So is it working now?'

'Oh yes. Working very well, isn't it Sally.'

'Works great. Even in low light.'

Ethan stopped eating and turned to Harry. 'So, hows things with you and the new girl?'

'Well, I texted her earlier, but she hasn't got back to me.'

'So, how did her hair get burned?'

He looked between Sally and Ethan who were both stifling a laugh.

His mother joined in. 'Yes, Harry, you still haven't told us what happened.'

'Doesn't really matter, Sally fixed it.'

Ethan was laughing a bit now causing Sally to join in.

'This was afterwards I assume,' he managed to get out between laughs.

Harold looked bemused. 'Am I missing something here? After what?'

'After we had been to the pub, dad,' Harry said.

Ethan winked at him.

Harry's phone pinged. As he got it out, his mum tutted.

'You know full well no phones at the diner table.'

'Sorry mum but this is important.' He left the table and went up to his room.

Harry returned with a smile on his face. 'She wants to see me tonight.'

There was tittering around the table. His father broke the silence.

'Well, I hope you you don't go back to the salon tonight.'

With that everybody except Harry burst into peels of laughter.

'I should have known you couldn't keep it to yourself Ethan.'

Ethan was almost crying with laughter.

'How much did you say?'

His mum, who hadn't been laughing as much as the others spoke.

'They told me a lot more than I ever wanted to know about my son's eh fornification.'

'Fornication,' Harry corrected.

'Call it what you want, I don't want to know about it.'

Mother then excused herself and went off to dish out the main meal, while the rest tried to compose themselves.

'Harry, you know our old bedsit.'

'The one you and Ethan rent out.'

'Yes, well, the tenant contacted us this morning and told us he is leaving in a month to move in with his boyfriend. So we thought if you wanted to rent it, it's yours.'

Before he could even think about it a loud clapping could be heard from the kitchen.

'Oh, that would be brilliant. I will need to think about it, mum and dad would miss me being about the house,' he said, tongue firmly in cheek.

Mum appeared at the kitchen door.

'Wouldn't you mum?'

'I would be heart broken. When are you leaving?'

'Also, you know how you said you could do with earning more money. Well, we, Ethan and I, thought you could work part-time and go to college the rest of the time to do a barbering course and learn to cut hair. Gents, of course. We would still pay you your full wage. After you are trained you could then have a chair in my salon.'

'Ow sis, that's brilliant, you are a lifesaver. Again.'

Ethan, king of the winkers, winked again and said, 'Oh and there is no CCTV in the bedsit. Not yet, anyway.'

This time they all laughed. Except mum, who could be heard singing in the kitchen.

Harry stood outside the sports bar. When Martina's fathers car drew up he was prepared to run. However, it was only Martina that got out before it drove off.

Harry knew when they kissed that this was the woman of his dreams.

'Harry, before we go in there is something I need to tell you. I told my parents the full story and that it was all my fault. I know I said his bark was worse than his bite but he said he was so angry he nearly thumped you.'

'Well, I got some great news today too. My sister has a bedsit she lets out. Her tenant is leaving next month and I am moving in. I know it's a bit sudden and we haven't been going together long but I would like you to move in with me.'

'What you mean like get engaged?'

'No! No, we don't need to be engaged to move in together.'

'I am only winding you up.'

'God, you had me going there.'

'Oh, what am I like. Wait a minute, this is a leap year, I could ask you.'

'No. If I am going to get married I will be doing the asking but it will be when the time is right. Tell you what, why not move in together and if we last a month, I will ask you. Deal?'

'Deal.' And they sealed it with a kiss.

GORDON'S STORY

GORDON Spencer was the owner of The Paint Depot, an independent paint warehouse, situated in an industrial estate. Today was the first day back after the Christmas holidays, being hands on with the business he personally welcomed the staff back after the Christmas holidays.

The staff, John, Derek, Colin, Amy and Lulu were seated in the canteen as instructed.

'Right, people, before we start work, I have an announcement to make.'

Colin, always the worrier, interjected. 'Are we closing?'

'No, Colin. We have never been busier.'

'Are we getting taken over. Rumour has it B and Q want to buy us.'

'News to me, Colin. Now if you listen and don't talk you might find out what I have to tell you.'

Colin sulked. A 40 year old man sulking doesn't look nice.

'What I have to tell you is that Cassie and I have split up. So if you have any views, want to tell me you told me so, or any other advice, come to me. Tell me to my face. I would prefer that than tittle tattle behind my back. Okay.'

There were murmurings from the crew but nobody said they would do as asked.

Derek, the king of the puns, had to comment. 'Gordon, it was nice of you not to gloss over it.' This was met by serious groaning.

'Predictable Derek. Right, the new campaign for the New Year starts today. 3 for 2 on all paint. That is on all paint. The big chains put conditions on their offers, some paint, usually the dearest, are exempt. Not us. Colin, your mission is to clear all the paint remover stock. We are changing to a new supplier next month and they don't want us to have any of their rivals gear on the shelves. Reduce it if you have to, just clear the shelves. Right, if there are no questions, lets get out there and sell paint.'

The staff file out, muttering as they go, leaving Gordon and John, the store manager.

'Don't say I told you so.'

'But.'

'Yes, you told me so but we had 10 years together and it was a bloody good 10 years. Come on, anybody, given the chance, would bite your hand off for the chance of screwing somebody 30 years younger.   '

'Unless they were 35.'

'Close to the bone, John. Right, what I should have said was anybody who is 55 would love to screw their 25 year old secretary.'

'Screw yes, but marry, no. The fact she gave you a blow job at her interview should have made it clear she was after more than a job.'

'Naively, I thought she just fancied me.'

'So, Cassie is back on the market, then. Going with what you just said, I should leave Mavis and indulge my fantasy of shagging a younger woman.'

'No, Cassie is toxic. Sure the first 5 years were great but when she got what she wanted, our 2 boys, we were as good as over. The last 5 years we were living separate lives, just together for the sake of the kids. I moved out on Boxing Day. I already had bought a penthouse place in town. Two weeks and I've heard nothing from her, just waiting for her Vulture Lawyer to start circling.'

'So, bet that's put you off women for life. It would me.'

'No, I was straight onto a Dating App. Kissing Frogs it's called and I hope to be kissing one tonight.'

'A frog?'

'No, a lady. Well, a woman at least.'

'You have a date tonight. You are a glutton for punishment.'

'Booked up for a meal for 2 at The Feathers.'

'You will never learn, Gordon.'

The Feathers is an old world pub in the middle of town. All low beams, horse brass and real ale by the roaring fire.

Gordon showed Myra to her seat opposite him. Myra is in her 50's, probably about 10 years younger than Gordon. She has a pleasant round face and round just about everything else.

They had done the pleasantries then Gordon couldn't resist a dig.

'I hope you don't think I'm being cheeky but your photo on the App doesn't seem up to date.'

'Oh, and you weren't grey in yours.'

Gordon raised his glass in salute. 'Touche. Foods marvellous, I brought my staff here for our Christmas dinner.'

'My first time here,' Myra said. 'I don't each much, my last partner said I ate like a mouse.'

Gordon smiled as he thought her ex must have meant like a fucking great hippopotamouse, by the size of her.

Gordon couldn't get her out quick enough. She sat in his Mercedes Coupe and marvelled at the luxury. He was all about that, image. Flash car, dapper dresser, cologne, a little jewellery but what he wore was expensive.

Myra would never fit in that image. A sort of human troll, the sooner he was shot of her the better. She lived on the outskirts of town and the Merc made short work of the journey.

'Fancy coming in for a coffee?' she asked.

'No, I don't think I could eat or drink anything else, I'm stuffed.'

'Lucky you. Of course you could come in and,' she hesitated as if shy, 'stuff me.'

Gordon shuddered at the thought. 'The truth is, I have an

early rise in the morning.'

'I could help with that too, I could give you a rise tonight.' Myra licked her lips, trying to look sexy but she just looked scary.

'Some other time, maybe.'

Myra released her seatbelt and leaned in for a goodnight kiss. Eyes shut, lips puckered, she was ready for action. Gordon kissed her on the cheek. Realising that was all she was getting, she barged her way out of the car. She slammed the door shut so hard the whole car shook with the tremor.

'Goodnight then,' Gordon said mockingly.

Gordon and John had a meeting first thing every morning usually to talk about the business but today the topic was mainly Myra.

'What a nightmare last night was. Firstly, she was a lot bigger than advertised. Her Dating App picture was taken about 4 or 5 stone ago. We went to the Feathers. You know the size of portions there, well she had 3 courses, wolfed the lot, nearly took the pattern off the plate. Then when I drove her home she wanted another course, intercourse. She was well pissed when I refused to go in.'

'What, you mean, you didn't oblige?'

'No way. I was scared if she went down on me she would have scoffed the lot, left me looking like an Action Man, you know, with the smooth groin.'

'So, no second date then?'

'Definitely not. When I say she was big, she was Orca big. If you had a session with her, you would claim travelling time for getting round about her.'

'So, are you giving it a bye for a bit?'

'No way Jose. I have another date tonight.'

'You are definitely a glutton for punishment.'

They were interrupted by a knocking on the office door. Amy was waiting to come in. Gordon waved her in.

'Gordon, you know you said you would prefer us to talk to

you and not behind your back.'

Gordon nodded, wondering what was coming next.

'Well, there is a thing on the Internet from last night and I think it's about you.'

'About me?'

'It's an App called Rate My Date.'

'There is an App for that.'

'There is an App for practically anything. Very popular this one is.'

'Go on then, what does it say.'

Amy read from her phone. 'Heading is- Disastrous Date with Geriatric Gordon.'

'Me- geriatric. Cheeky cow.'

'Called me fatter than my photo yet his hair was pure grey while in his pic he was pure black. Didn't have the energy for any action either.'

'There won't be many people read that guff.'

'No, they have only about half a million members.'

'Half a million. Have people got nothing better to do than rate their date? Well, I will need to up my game.'

'It finishes with avoid at all costs.'

'Thanks Amy. Anyway, I have another chance to get my rating back up. Well, if I am Geriatric Gordon she must be Mammoth Myra.'

Gordon tried a different tack, this time opting for a Gastro pub. The atmosphere lively as people were there to enjoy others company not just put their snouts in the trough like last night. There were a few good looking women about the place but they would be for another night, tonight was Melanie's.

When she appeared, there were no problems with her and her photo. If anything she was prettier. She had long, blonde hair, nice features with accentuated make-up, nothing garish. In her 50's no doubt but her figure trim enough for her age. Gordon struggled not to stare at her chest, it was way out in front of her.

She could have fed a crèche with those puppies.

After the preliminaries, they settled down to a cosy corner. Gordon was on the orange juice again, Melanie asked for proseccco so he got her a bottle.

'Why the orange juice, you aren't on medication?'

For a second he wondered if she had read that Rate My Date crap and realised he was the but of the Moro's joke.

'No, I am driving. Can't drink on a work night. I run my own business.'

'Well, I hope that means you are taking me back home later, save me from getting a taxi.'

'I hope I am taking you home later.'

Melanie it turned out had been divorced for 11 years and had only a couple of relationships since. Gordon told her his circumstances and they spent a while cursing and slagging off their ex's.

All too soon, it seemed, the wine bottle was emptied and they were heading to Melanie's place.

Next morning, Gordon was in the office early. He was drinking strong, black coffee. John was surprised to see him, especially after a night out.

'Jesus, Gordon, you look a bit rough.'

'Oh, I am more than a bit rough. I am really rough.'

'You weren't drinking?'

'No, totally teetotal.'

'So, how are you rough?'

'My mate last night was called Melanie. She told me her school friends called her Melons. It wasn't really a nickname, it was a title she well and truly earned. I'm not exaggerating when I say they were the best boobs I have ever seen or played with. Natural too. God, I played with them for hours. She was also very fond of Oral and for a woman in her 50's it was very tidy down there. Not hanging out to much if you know what I mean. Man but could she take a pounding. Harder, faster, deeper. She kept saying it and I kept giving her it. Hours we were at it.'

'Right, that's enough.'

'John, I have never taken you for a prude.'

'No. I want you to stop for two reasons. One, I am so fucking jealous right now and two, I am starting to get a hard-on.'

'I stayed the night and we were at it again at 5 o'clock this morning.'

'You are going to kill yourself man.'

'But what a way to go, eh.'

'So, is she going to be a steady thing?'

'No. After we finished this morning, she thanked me for taking her out. Then she says she is a bit hard up at the moment. I felt like saying I was hard up a few minutes ago but really I felt a bit hurt. You know, as if I was paying for sex. So I only had 30 quid in my wallet so I gave her that.'

'What, do you think she is on the game?'

'No, just think, you know, good looking guy, well off, drives a Merc, must be loaded. Just wanted a few quid for the privilege.'

'So, after that you told her it was over?'

'No. You never say never.'

'So, what if she gives you a poor rating on Rate My Date?'

'Then I will give her a score for Value For Money.'

Later that day, the shop floor was quiet, all the staff were at the cash desk except Lulu who was in the office. Suddenly the tannoy broke into life.

'Telephone call for Mr. Vassell, line 1.'

Gordon headed into his office to take the call. There seemed to be a strange crackle from the tannoy. A door could be heard closing then Gordon's voice could be heard over the tannoy.

'Hello, Gordon Vassell speaking.'

'Hello tiger. How are you this morning?'

The staff all stare up at the speakers above them. Except John, who, realising Lulu had put the call through the tannoy, and rushed for the office.

'I'm tired.'

'I am a bit tender. You gave me a real pounding. Tonight, I want you again. Harder, deeper, faster.'

'Don't know if I can manage tonight. I am really busy at work.'

The staff were all chuckling among themselves. Derek interrupted by saying he couldn't manage in the Paint Store before Melanie spoke again.

'Oh, tiger, I want you to stroke my pussy.'

The tannoy then went quiet.

This time the staff burst out laughing among themselves. Derek again couldn't keep his mouth shut. 'Do you think Melanie had a cat?'

Colin looked pensive. 'Well if Gordon isn't available I will. I love stroking furry animals.'

John was talking to Lulu when Gordon stormed in.

'What the Hell happened there? Were you deliberately trying to humiliate me?'

Lulu started crying. Between bubbles she managed to speak.

'No. I was up all night with a migraine. I still don't feel well. I just got a bit mixed up.'

'Nothing worse than being up all night, is there Gordon,' John said, in her defence and trying to make light of it.

Gordon calmed himself a bit. All right, he hadn't taken on Lulu for her brains so it was partly his fault that she messed something like this up.

'God almighty, how much do you think that lot out there heard?'

'Not much really. Anyway, I am sure nobody will mention it.'

'Right, Lulu, if you don't feel well, take the rest of the day off. John can stay in here and man the switchboard. But do not tell that lot anything. That way they will think you have been sacked and they will maybe keep quiet about it.'

Gordon tackled the tannoy issue head on by having a meeting the next morning before work. The workforce were all in the canteen as ordered.

'Everybody is here, so I will begin. Now I take it after the tannoy incident that you think of me as some laughing stock?'

There was shaking of heads or no reaction around the table.

'No comment? Well, Lulu assured me it was a genuine mistake and I have accepted that.'

Lulu kept looking down, accepting her rebuke.

'However, if any of you think it is funny to make a fool of me, I will not hesitate to sack you.'

There was a stunned silence now. Not only because of what he said it was also the tone of his voice.

'Anybody want to say anything?'

Amy cleared her throat. 'I take it you didn't go out last night.'

'Not that it's any of your business but I stayed in and had an early night in bed. Alone!'

'Oh, it's just that your other date, Melanie put a rating for you.'

'Go on.'

'Well, she calls you Gordon the Gigolo.' She reads from her phone. 'Knows the way around a woman's body. Although the black hair is now silver. He is still a silver fox, though.'

'Well, it's great what 30 pounds gets you.'

This lead to puzzled looks around the table.

'Well, if there is nothing else, lets sell paint.'

The workers filed out leaving Gordon and John.

'Well, I will need to make amendments to my App picture. So I will be late in tomorrow. Okay with you, you can cope.'

John's laughter was his answer.

Gordon walked into the store next morning with his usual arrogant swagger. His silver hair was back to raven black of years past. As he walks through the store the staff all look mesmerised.

As he walks past the paint remover display his good mood evaporated. Grabbing the sign he barges back to the office, scanning the store for Colin.

The sign is dumped on John's desk.

'What the fuck is this?' Before John could answer he shouted through to Lulu- ' Get Colin in here.' The tannoy echoes with 'Colin Preston report to the manager's office.'

'Gordon.'

'Save it,' Gordon said, not giving John a chance to explain. 'When he comes in here, I want you to sack him!'

'What's wrong with you? Yesterday it was Lulu you wanted to sack, today Colin. Will it be me tomorrow? I think you are looking at this the wrong way.'

Gordon pointed to the sign. 'No, I am looking at it the right way.'

Colin knocks and enters the office. Gordon hasn't calmed any.

'What the fuck is this about?' He lifted the sign.

'You wanted the paint stripper sold and I came up with this advert.'

'Our stripper works HARDER, It penetrates DEEPER And removes paint FASTER. Are you going to tell me this isn't a wind-up.'

'No, it isn't. You see, when you gave me the task of selling the stripper, I couldn't come up with anything. Didn't sleep on Monday night. Then after your phone call, it stuck in my head. Harder, deeper, faster. Round and round it went and I came up with the sign.'

'Did Derek or any of the rest of them put you up to this?'

'No, it's all my own work.'

John again tries to talk but Gordon raised a hand to keep him quiet. John he gets up from his chair so quick it falls behind him with a crash.

This focused everyone's attention.

'Gordon, will you listen to me now., I've been trying to tell you. Colin showed me this first thing this morning. I was dubious at first because I knew your reaction but I said we would try it until lunchtime. But guess what? We sold 6 units already. We hardly sold 6 units all last year, that's why we are changing supplier. As they say, it pays to advertise.'

'A £120 worth this morning.'

The other two nodded.

'Well, what are you waiting for Colin? Get that sign back up. Oh, and good work.'

Colin left with precious sign, leaving Gordon and John.

'Why would you just not speak to me?'

'I know I lost it. Since Cassy and I split I've really been on edge. I know she is going to take me to the cleaners but I was more worried about getting another suitable woman. Then yesterday and now this. I thought it was a wind-up.'

'Colin might seem slow but as you see, he gets there in the end.'

'Harder, deeper, faster. It is quite catchy. Hope Melanie doesn't come in the store, she will claim royalties. She will be after more money off me. Speaking of which and talk about it paying to advertise, since Melanie posted about the Geriatric Gigolo my app's been red hot.'

'So, no more Melanie then?'

'No. Once again, you were right. She would have killed me. No, I need some-one a bit eh slower.'

'More your age.'

'Oh, God no. More my sex drive.'

'Older then.'

'Funny guy. Do you want sacked?'

'Well, while I am in the bad books, I will just come out with it. What's with the hair?'

'I got that stuff for men, you know hides greys. Well I put it on then dozed off. You should leave it 20, 30 minutes max. I must have slept for an hour. Now, it won't stop glowing black.'

'I thought you were going for another go at Melanie and were taking the morning off to recover.'

'No. I had to go round to the house and get the rest of my stuff. Cassy burst out laughing when she saw my hair. As you can imagine, we are well and truly over.'

'Maybe you should give the dating scene a rest.'

'Are you kidding? My stock is high and so am I. No, tonight I am seeing Cathy.

Gordon decided on The Anchorage for his rendezvous with Cathy. Gordon sat at the bar and escorted Cathy to a secluded table when she arrived. She was very pleasant on the eye.

'I know it's corny but do you come here often?'

'Last month I moved to a flat just round the corner from here. Since then it's been my regular. Nice in here.'

'Yes. Not any yobs.'

'No, expensive enough to keep the young neds out. So, I take it you read about me on Rate My Date.' Quiz night's good, some really smart cookies. The food's top nosh too. You sure you don't want anything to eat?'

'No. The plan was this was just a drink to get to know each other.'

'Oh, sure. The thing I want to know is if you read about me on Rate My Date?'

'Yes, I was intrigued. Were you Geriatric Gordon or the Geriatric Gigolo? I was also amazed you were so honest about Myra.'

'Well I didn't say she was fat to her face, I was more subtle than that. However, she had more chins than a Chinese phone book. The thing was she took the huff because I wouldn't go in for coffee. And by coffee, I don't mean coffee. '

Cathy was laughing. Her face seemed to light up when she

laughed, before she seemed to Gordon like somebody who carried a lot of hurt about in her heart. No, we though wasn't the time to pursue that.

'So, Gordon, how do I rate against my photo?'

'Honestly?'

'It's best to be honest from the start.'

'You actually look better than your photo. You were attractive not glammed up but now with your hair and make-up done, I don't have the words to describe it without sounding corny. All I can say is there is nothing not to like about you.'

'God, any more of that and you will have me blushing.'

'Well, you certainly look like your photo now, with the black hair.'

'Oh, this. I had a disaster with the hair dye. Put it on then fell asleep.'

Cathy started laughing. To Gordon, she laughed like somebody who hadn't had much to laugh about for a while. She would look at his shiny Barnet then burst out laughing again. Her laughing stopped when a dark figure appeared in the doorway. When she acknowledged him, he backed out.

'Oh, that's my taxi.'

'We will need to do this again.'

'Yes. How about lunch tomorrow?'

'Yes, great. Let me know later where you would like to go and I will book it.'

They kissed goodnight, a gentle peck on the cheek and Cathy left, turning at the front door to blow Gordon a kiss. He caught it and blew it back. God, what was he turning into.

Gordon was in the office before John the next morning. The coffee pot was full and the heady smell filled the room.

John was wrapped up for the cold weather. By the time he removed all his outer layers, the owner had his coffee and biscuits ready for him at his desk.

'Chocolate biccies, what's the occasion. Celebrating?'

'Yes.'

'Was this the date last night.'

Gordon nodded but his smile told more.

'Good, was it?'

'Better than good. Very, very good.'

'Spend the night, did we?'

'No. Cathy isn't that kind of women. She is the kind that needs to be loved before there is anything physical.'

'Wow.'

'What do you mean wow? Do you think I am incapable of a deep and meaningful relationship?'

'Well, for me it would be your first.'

'No, second. I was truly, madly and deeply in love with my first wife. Unfortunately I didn't match up to the personal trainer I suggested she went to and I paid for. Practically paid him to fuck her then she fucked me over. Financially that is.'

'And this Cathy isn't like that?'

'No. But there is something in her past that has hurt her and she hasn't opened up to me about it yet.'

'So, has this super Cathy got a surname.'

'Yes. It's Cathy Dunning.'

'Cathy Dunning. I know that name. Where do I know that name from? Somewhere in the past I am sure. It will come to me. So, when is the next date?'

'We are going out for lunch today.'

Gordon sat waiting for Cathy at the bar of The Corinthian. In it's day it had been the premier place to eat in town but sadly the standards had slipped. Still nice and pricey.

Cathy walked in and Gordon felt his heart skip a beat. Suddenly he was a 15 year old at the 4th year disco, dancing with Helen Peacock. Helen had been wearing a boob tube and had more than enough bust to keep it up comfortably. Unfortunately she only agreed to go to the disco with him to make Andy Sharp jealous. Come the slow dances and Gordy was dumped for Andy.

Even in a headscarf and waterproof jacket Cathy looked stunning. Peeling them off, she was wearing a floral dress and red shoes.

They kissed gently on the cheek. Her scent was subtle but sensuous. That summed her up to him, everything about her was subtle and sensuous.

Gordon had asked for a window seat and the waiter showed them to their table. From the moment they sat down it was as if they were continuing from the previous evenings date.

The moment spoiled when Gordon's phone beeped. He had set the ringtones up so that he knew who it was. It was John's signal that beeped. The only way he would messages him while at lunch would be if it was very important.

Cathy could read from Gordon's face that the beep troubled him.

'Problem?'

'It's my store manager. Sorry, but I better look.'

The message read simply- Call me ASAP, and out of ear-shot.

'Oh, dear, problem with an order. I really need to call him right away. Sorry. '

'Oh, that's okay.'

'Best go outside. In case the language gets a bit fruity.'

Gordon walked out of the hotel. As he left the building he thought to himself that it better be as important as he thought or he would need to take John down a peg or two, manager or not.

John's mobile was answered on the first ring.

'Well.'

'Remember I said it would come to me.'

'What? This isn't the time for riddles.'

'Cathy. Cathy Dunning. It just dawned on me who she is. That's her maiden name, her married name is Cathy McQuade. She is wife of Jo Jo McQuade, currently residing at Her Majesty's pleasure, probably in high security.'

'Her ex husband is a gangster.'

'Nothing ex about him.'

Gordon looked up at the window, Cathy watched pensively. Gordon gave her a re-assuring wave while at the same time his guts were collapsing.

'Okay, thanks for the heads up. See you soon.'

Gordon returned and tried to continue the date in the same manner while all sorts of wild and wacky thoughts were zooming around his head.

'What are your plans for Sunday?' he asked.

'I'm free. My social calender is quite empty this weather. '

'Okay, if I asked you what your ideal date would be, anything, what would it be?'

'I always loved picnics. You know, the tartan rug, the flasks of barely drinkable tea and coffee. Sandwiches with the crusts cut off, all that.'

'January isn't the best month for picnic's.'

The both laughed, especially as a shower of rain whipped up and rattled against the window next to them.

'Right, tell you what, meet me outside the station on Sunday at noon.'

'All very mysterious.'

Gordon walked into the office without the spark he had left with.

'Are you sure you have the right Cathy?' Although he said it, deep down he knew John was correct.

John motioned him over to his computer. On the screen were Jo Jo McQuade and his wife entering the court for his trial. It was Cathy. His Cathy. A bit younger looking and pale and drawn compared to how she was now.

'That's that, then.'

Gordon never spoke for a few minutes then asked. 'Where will I get 3 metres square of astro turf?'

High noon on Sunday at the station. The rain was off although the black clouds above threatening more rain soon. Gordon stood at the station entrance wearing a Hawaiian shirt, shorts, trainers and holding an umbrella over his head.

Cathy got out of a taxi resplendent in a large raincoat and waterproof hat and sand shoes. She was carrying a large beach bag.

They came together in a warm embrace, hard to do in the chill wind. They kissed and smiled before breaking.

Cathy walked in towards the station. Gordon took her hand and led her the other way, away towards the river.

'Where are we going?'

'Not far. You will know when you get there.'

Down at the waterside, they continued until they came to the waterside apartments. Gordon then led her round to the entrance way. Inside there were 2 lifts, one marked general, the other penthouse.

Gordon's key summoned the lift.

'Is this your place?'

Gordon smiled and nodded. Nobody else had made it over his new abode's threshold, this was a special day.

The lift opened out into a small corridor then a fancy glass door.

Inside they were met by what felt like a wall of heat.

Cathy took off her rain wear and was also in shorts and t-shirt.

'Is it always this warm?'

'No but you don't go on a picnic when it's cold.'

The living room was lit up with every possible source being switched on.

Cathy laughed when she saw the picnic site. Gordon had laid out a square of astro grass and had placed a tartan rug on it. Beside it was a picnic basket and a bottle of champagne, chilling in a bucket.

Cathy beamed at the site. 'It's, it's perfect.'

'Nothings too good for you.'

They kissed again.

'Think you better turn the heat down, either that or we will end up naked or asleep.

'I know what I would prefer,' Gordon said as he walked over to the thermostat.

They sat on the rug and ate of the feast he had prepared and quaffed the ice cold champagne.

'When I was a kid, I dreamed of a picnic like this.'

'It's never too late to have a dream come true.'

'You are such a nice man.'

'Nice?'

'Lovely. Gorgeous. Sexy. Clever and nice. Does that describe you?'

'Getting there. I could say the same for you.'

After the food and drink, Cathy said it was sunbathing time. She went in her bag and pulled out her two piece suit. 'I will just nip to the toilet.'

'Sorry, but there aren't toilets at a picnic.'

'Right, I am going over here to change. No peeking.'

Gordon turned his back but managed to angle his sitting to catch a glimpse of her in a mirror on the fire wall. As she stripped off, Gordon suddenly felt like some kind of perve and looked down at his feet. Trainers. He untied his trainers and popped off his trainer socks.

If he was sunbathing he would take off his shirt so off it came.

Cathy sprayed a bit more perfume on then lay next to Gordon on the blanket.

'It's so quiet here. I could sleep.'

'Yes, forty winks would be nice.'

Due to the combination of the heat and the champagne, Gordon must have nodded off. He was wakened by something was tickling his face. He struggled to open his eyes at first then couldn't focus at what was hitting his face. It took him a few seconds to realise it was a bra strap. He smiled as he remembered they were having a picnic.

Turning round he found Cathy topless and on her side, smiling.

'Hello you.'

'Hello yourself. I think you are due a wee reward for this picnic.'

She leaned in and kissed him. The kissing continued and Gordon brought his hand up to cup her breast. Her nipple stiffened almost to the touch. There was no objection, just more kissing. His hand travelled down to her bikini bottoms. There was enough give for him to slip his hand down and feel her sex. Cathy meantime had a hand in his shorts preparing him for what she, they, wanted next.

Gordon slipped off his shorts while Cathy slid her bottoms off. Gordon lay on top and in an instant they were making love. Gordon had slept with so many women over the years but this was so different. Cathy had such control of her pubic muscles that it was as if she would take him to the brink then relax them enough for him to pound her rhythmically. After a perfect love-making sessions he felt the heat building and knew he was close to climaxing. Cathy came at the same time as him and they lay back, spent.

When they got their breaths back, Cathy wrapped her half of the blanket round her. Gordon did likewise and they met in the middle.

Cathy turned to him with tears in her eyes. 'That was lovely. This afternoon has been perfect. Shame there is a big bad World outside the door. You know, I wish I could sell everything and disappear. Go abroad, Portugal or Spain.'

Gordon thought for a minute then swallowed hard.

'You know he would still find you.'

With those 7 words, Cathy's perfect day crashed and burned.

'You know. When did you find out?'

'Yesterday at lunch. The phone call was from my manager

who remembered you from the old days.'

'But you still brought me here.'

'Everything I said about you being special I meant. However, I know it could never be with us, we could never be together forever. However I wanted a piece of that magic.'

'I know. It was a crazy dream, thinking I could go dating with Jo Jo inside.'

'Do you want me to drive you home?'

'In a while. When the picnic is over. Then I would like you to take me to bed.'

Gordon drove slowly to the outskirts of town. The date had been perfect and if it lasted a bit longer all the better. Cathy had been quiet since they got out of bed. Now she only spoke to give directions. It was dark and the streets quiet, the journey was quicker than Gordon wanted it to be.

'Just down here on the left.'

Gordon started his indicator and slowed.

'Shit no, drive on!' With that, she slid down in her seat, out of sight.

Gordon did as he was told.

'What is it?'

'It's who is it. Billy Delaney. Jo Jo's eyes and ears on the outside. Well, as far as I am concerned. His car is in the drive. Take a left here and stop.'

Cathy took out her phone and called some-one.

'Irene, has Billy been in touch?'

'Shit, okay. No. No problem. Catch you later.'

'Right, do you know the Drivers Arms?'

'Yes. Look is everything all right.'

'Oh, it will be. Just drop me there. I will phone Billy and get him to pick me up there.'

'Will he not tell Jo Jo?'

'He would but I won't let him. I will get a couple of drinks in him then seduce him. Then he won't be able to tell Jo Jo anything.'

'You are incorrigible. Supposing he doesn't go for it?'

'I know the way he looks at me he would think it was all his Christmas' rolled into one. After a few drinks, I will show him the negligee I bought for the old man's coming out surprise. Then flash the gash and he will be up there like a rat up a drain pipe.'

Gordon drove on, this time he was quiet.

He parked up along the street from the Drivers. They kissed goodbye.

'If only things had been different, Cathy.'

'Que sera sera, whatever will be will be.'

With that she got out of the car and walked out of his life.

Gordon and John are in the office before the Monday meeting.

'Finished with Cathy yesterday.'

'Yesterday? I told you on Friday. You were quiet when you returned on Friday I thought you had already dumped her.'

'No. I took her on a picnic yesterday and after it, took her home.'

'So, you didn't, you know?'

'Oh yes, I did. Twice. And it was absolutely amazing.'

'Worth dying for?'

'Probably. It won't come to that, she was going to fix things when I dropped her off.'

'How do you mean?'

'You don't want to know. One thing is for sure, I won't be doing any more dating for a while.'

Five weeks later and there was a lot of gossip as Gordon and John walked into the canteen for the Monday meeting.

'So, what's the buzz?'

'Have you not heard? Jo Jo McQuade was released on

prison on Friday,' Amy gushed.

'Was he not in for 10 to 15 years?' John asked on his boss' behalf.

'It was but his lawyers got him out on appeal,' Amy went on. 'Anyway, turns out a lot of his money was invested in paintings, statues and the like in the house. Turns out his wife, Cathy and her driver Billy Delaney, sold all the good stuff and have disappeared. Talk is they went to Spain.'

Gordon was quiet as he digested this information. Then questions came into his head. If she had been serious when they were together why did she not come to him? Was Billy a better love-maker. So many things were swirling about in his head. Then he realised all eyes were on him.

'Wouldn't like to be in their shoes when he catches up with them from what I heard about this Jo Jo guy. Anyway, this gossiping won't sell paint. John, what's on this week.'

John then issues the orders for the week.

After the meeting everybody filed out except Gordon and John.

'Well, that was a turn up. Lets you off the hook, big time.'

'You know, I thought we had something special. Something very special. I thought she would have come to me if she was thinking of running away.'

'Would you have gone?'

'It's a hypothetical question but yes, I think I would have. Wouldn't have gone to Spain, first place they would look. Central America would have been my destination. Que sera sera. Anyway, back playing the field, where's my phone?'

Wednesday night and Gordon is waiting in Ricky's Bar and Grill. For the past 5 weeks he had been sitting at home twiddling his thumbs. It felt good to get back on the woman trail. He was quite excited about the arrival of Sonia. Her picture showed a strong woman, with a very distinctive hairstyle.

Sonia breezed in. She had the look of a woman who knew

what she wanted.

Sonia's silver hair was shaved on one side and flopped down the other. Her lips vibrant red stood out more with her pale make-up. She was wearing a white t-shirt and leather waistcoat. Her bare arms showed a tattoo on her left arm.

They air kissed twice and Gordon directed her to a table away from the bar which was quite noisy. Sonia asked for a G and T so Gordon went to the bar.

As he waited to be served he could see other men at the bar glimpsing and admiring Sonia.

When he returned with her drink and his orange juice Sonia looked disappointed.

'Orange juice? Do you not drink?'

'Not when I am working the next morning.'

'Oh, that's good. Thought you might have been an alcoholic.'

'Jesus, Is it suddenly against the Law to have a soft drink? You aren't the first person to ask me that, do I look like an alcoholic?'

'No, but every other guy I've been out with drank alcohol. Most of them too much. God, I hope that doesn't make me sound like a slapper, as if I have been out with a lot of men.'

'So, how many? Sorry, that's maybe not a question for a first date. It's just that my last 3 dates were less than economical with the truth.'

'No, it's okay. Anyway, this is my first date this year. Too fussy I think. Anyway, last year I had only 4 dates. Never got past the first date with any of them.'

'Your choice?'

'No, well not all the time. First guy dumped me by text half an hour after our date. The second one had tattoo's all over his face. I like tattoos but on the face, pretty scary. Another looked like a sex offender so I kicked him to touch and the last one, when I took him back to my place, I think he fancied my husband more than me.'

'Your husband?'

'It's a bit of a strange situation. We are separated but still live together. We are trapped with our mortgage situation. With what we have to pay neither of us can afford to go their own way. Our house has been on the market for 18 months but nobody seems interested.'

'I'm intrigued. So, how do you share it?'

'Oh, we have our own bedrooms and share the kitchen and bathroom. I can bring fellows back on a Tuesday, Thursday and Saturday, he gets Monday, Wednesday and Friday.'

'So, have you taken many men back?'

'God no, just the one that fancied him.'

'Does he bring women back?'

'Oh yes. I think he gets them from the pound, the dogs he brings back. I think he does it either to make me jealous or to make me feel sorry for him and that I will take him back.'

'And will you?'

'No, never! Since we got married he has been after every bit of skirt he can lay his dirty hands on. Just looking at him now makes my skin crawl.'

'Is there no sign of the house getting sold?'

'No, we have never even had a second viewing. I think he sabotages the viewings and he won't let me show people around.'

The DJ announces that the quiz would start in 10 minutes.

'Do you fancy the quiz?'

'Oh God, no. Simon used to drag me out every week to our local pub quiz every week. He would argue over every question, put down his answer then blame me when it was wrong.'

'Sounds like a proper cunt.'

'You are right, he is a proper cunt.'

'So, what do you want to do, fancy going for something to eat?'

'Wouldn't mind a bit of food.'

'Well, we could go to The Golden Wok and sit in or grab a carry out and go back to my place.'

'Is it far?'
'About 200 yards.'
'Sounds cosier.'

Gordon and Sonia walk into Gordon's pad. Sonia looks round well impressed.

'Wow, this is some place. Must have cost a fortune.'

'Oh, it's not mine, belongs to a mate who is working in Hong Kong at the moment. My last wife left me practically homeless. Fortunate for me he lets me live here rent free,'

Gordon didn't really know why he lied to Sonia. Maybe he was scared she would think he was some kind of sugar daddy or fancied moving in here to get away from her cunt of a husband.

'Where is the toilet? I need to freshen up.'

'It's through to the left, second door.'

Gordon busied himself with dishing out the food in the open plan kitchen. He sat the bowls on the breakfast bar. More intimate when eating than sat apart at the dinner table.

Gordon tasted one of the prawns. God, those guys could do magic with a wok and a bit of sauce.

Gordon walked through to the hallway.

'It's getting cold!' he shouted. He then noticed the bathroom door was open and the light was off.

He walked down the corridor and found the master bedroom door ajar. He knew he had left it closed. Pushing the door open, the room was in darkness but the shaft of light showed Sonia sitting up in the bed. The sheets covered her bottom half but above them she was naked. Gordon then saw that her clothes were sitting neatly piled at the bottom of the bed.

'Are you coming to join me? I haven't had a man for over 18 months and I need a good shag.'

Gordon was already taking his clothes off. 'Wasn't that hungry anyway. The food will reheat.'

They kissed and cuddled and with Sonia's encouragement he entered her.

All the time they were coupling, all Gordon could think of was how different it was since the last twice with Cathy. She worked her body to pleasure a man. Sonia, for her good looks and taut body, just lay there and let him take his pleasure.

As he lay beside her she was smiling as if it had been great. Gordon, however, suspected he had found the reason for her husbands dalliances, she was a crap ride.

Gordon parked his car directly outside Sonia's house as directed. They glimpsed up and saw the upstairs curtains twitching. Sonia leaned over and kissed Gord. Her tongue snaked in his mouth a lot more than it had at his place. Was she turned on knowing her hubby was watching, Gordon wondered.

'Are you sure you will be all right?'

'Yes. He will probably be pulling away in his room by now. The thing is that he will be thinking about me differently now. Now that I am desirable to somebody else he will want me all the more. Before you say anything else I know this is it. There is somebody else in your heart.'

'How,' was all he managed to get out.

'Your body language after we had been to bed. You tried to hide it but after living with that lying, cheating cunt in there I know when somebody means what they are saying.'

'Sorry.'

'No, don't be sorry. I am really glad I met you tonight. Good food, good company and the sex reminded me what certain bits of my body are for.'

They looked up again and the curtains twitched again.

'Once more for the audience Sonia,' Gordon said then leaned over and kissed her again.

There followed more tonsil tennis then Sonia got out of the car and she too walked out of his life.

Gordon sat at his desk next morning.

'Bad night?' John asked as he entered the office.

'Took Sonia to the pub. Back to mine and in bed before 8.

Bit of food, back to bed then dropped her back home afterwards.'

'So, why the face like a smacked arse.'

'Well, the sex wasn't great. But the main thing was, she isn't Cathy.'

'Cathy? I thought you were over her.'

'I thought I was too.'

JIMMY'S STORY

'LADIES and Gentlemen, put your hands together for Jimmy Caldwell.'

Jimmy's hands were sweating so much the mike nearly slid out of his grip. He tried to walk slowly as if it was second nature but he was absolutely cacking himself. First professional stand up gig. Sure he had done plenty of amateur stints but he was actually getting paid for this.

The lights shining on the stage meant the audience were mostly anonymous to him, save for the front row, which he hoped would help.

'Good evening Paisley!'

'It's fucking Glasgow you prick!' some wag shouted.

'That was the joke!'

'Wisnae funny,' was the retort.

It fell flatter than a 90 year old's tit. Absolute tumble-weed moment. Fuck, fuck, fuck, he thought. Need to get them laughing now or he would be booed off.

'Get on with it,' somebody said with venom in it.

'Woman phones her hubby says I've knocked down a pig and I think it's dead. Are you sure it's dead, he asks. He hears a bang and she says he is now. But what do I do with the panda car?'

This got a few laughs and he was away. People always like Police jokes.

'Scottish Siamese twins wrote a book, called it Oor Wullie. Woman walks into a chemists and asks if they sell extra large durex. The assistant says they do so she sits down next to the counter. Do you want to buy any she was asked? No, she says, I will just wait here and see who buys them.'

There were laughs now but Jimmy suddenly realised he was talking too quick and not pausing between jokes. At least now he was getting a few laughs, he was getting them on his side.

At Stand-Up school he was told to take a bottle of water with him on stage. This wasn't just a prop it was also a tool to use. Stop and take a break, sip of water. Let the audience enjoy their laugh. Then onto the next joke.

'I've not been lucky with the girls.'

There were few heckles but because they spoke at the same time he didn't hear them specifically.

'Last girlfriend was a bit of an anal boxer, she'd been battered about the ring.'

This took a few moments to sink in and was met with mix of groans and laughs.

'Girl before that had a mouth like a bird cage, it had seen a cock a too.'

Same reaction but at least they didn't boo.

Another thing at Stand-Up school he learned was to tell jokes people could take away with them and use as their own with friends or workmates. Those were two. Time for a longer one.

'Woman goes and buys a dress for her husbands works dance. She thinks he will go ape-shit because it cost 600 quid. So, she makes him a steak dinner, can of lager, Vienetta for afters, the works. Posh as fuck eh. Then she goes up and changes and walks in with the dress on. You look lovely he says. Then she tells him the price. Give us a twirl, he says and she turns round. Your panties are coming down, he says. She checks and laughs. No they are not. For 600 quid he says, you bet they are.'

That got laughs and a few groans, the men laughing and woman groaning he guessed.

To finish he thought he would tell one of his true tales.

'As you might have guessed, this isn't my full time job.'

'You aren't joking,' somebody shouted.

'I went to the job centre and had an interview. They asked
if I could perform under
pressure but I said no, didn't know the words but I could do a bit
of Bohemian Rhapsody.'

Pause for laugh. 'They didn't laugh either. So I said I
wanted to work with people. Great they said, school crossing patrol. I said I'm too young for that, I'm only 23. What they said
next really inspired me to take the job. Five words, we will stop
your money. As I walked away I thought it could have a lot of
potential. Sure I have to put up with a lot of snotty brats but each
one has a mum with them.'

'Any yummy mums out there?'

A few shouts as the mums, enjoying a few precious hours
away from the kids and getting full of drink, shout loudly.

'Well, I get gumsy grans. One day I was propositioned. It
was after the lunchtime session and it was a warm day. Fancy
coming back to mine for a cuppa? Of course I was naive enough
to think a cup of tetley was in order. Now the woman had sports
pants, a sports hat and sunglasses. I thought she was one of the
kids mums. So we walked up to hers. Arm in arm. No sooner had
she closed the front door behind us then she had me jammed
against the back of the door and had her mouth clamped over
mine. I started to respond but soon got a taste of old ashtray. It
was fucking horrible. Then she took the glasses and cap off and
she must have been 60 if she was a day. Her face was more wrin-
kled than my scrotum. I mean I am only 23 and want experience
but not with likes of her.'

'You know the type lads, body off Baywatch, face off
Crimewatch.'

Pause and a drink of water.

'Next thing, she pulls me through to her bedroom. She lay
on the bed and pulled her pants down. Suddenly this huge mass
of grey pubes appeared between her legs. It was as if she had Don
King the boxing promoter down there. If you don't know him,
Google it. I stared in disbelief. Big mistake, she grabbed my coat
and with amazing strength managed to grab me and propel me

towards her. Next thing I knew my nose was in the middle of her pubes. Well I thought the smell of her breath was bad but this was off the scale. It was what I imagined the toilet door in a fishing smack would smell like.'

Another paused but this time it was a mix of groans and laughs.

'From your groans some of you have been there. Somehow I managed to escape her grasp and I got out from her house and ran all the way home. Now, I was wearing my crossing patrol jacket that's like a giant, heavy, white bin bag so by the time I got home I was drenched in sweat. So I stripped off and wrapped a towel around myself as I tried to cool down. Next thing, I got a knock on the front door. Without thinking, I opened it. There was my afternoon tea partner. She must have followed me like some Terminator style rampant granny striding after me. So, next thing she is on top of me, my towel thrown in a corner and her howking her pants down enough for entry. Think I was traumatised because I just lay there as she enjoyed my body. Next thing, the back door opened and my mum walked in carrying a basket of washing. What the hell is going on here she shouted?' 'You were exactly the same at school, brillo pubes said. Thickest in class. Well, mum said, maybe it was because you were a crap teacher.'

Another drink of water as the audience laughed.

'That's my time up, Ladies and Gents, just to let you know, if there are any Stand-Up
groupies in tonight, I will be in the bar after the show.'

Jimmy was buzzing as he walked into the bar at the front of the venue. His original plan had been to shoot off, get the first available train home but the adrenalin was still coursing through his veins. He was too hyper to head home, needed to chill a bit. So he got a pint of lager and sat at a table on his own. He got out his notebook started to write down what he felt went well and what didn't. He hadn't started well but that was, he felt, down to nerves. The water bottle worked well, taking breaks gave the audience a chance to laugh.

He checked his phone. A message from Karen, his girlfriend. Phoned your mum to see how you were. LYING. Telling me you were ill so you could go to a gig instead of going out with me. The last straw Jimmy. I hope you and Stand-Up will be happy together.

He tried to phone but went straight to her answer machine. Dumped by text, the story of his life. Tonight of all nights, when things were going his way for once.

'Excuse me, can I get you a drink?'

Jimmy looked up and saw a very pretty blond looking down at him.

'I just got one,' he replied, motioning to the almost full pint in front of him.

'I saw your act, I thought you were very funny. In fact, you have been the best tonight.'

'Thanks. Can I get you a drink?'

'Vodka and tonic, please.'

Jimmy went to the bar and looked over at the girl, now seated at the table he had just left. Way out of his league, girlfriend-wise but it would be good to get a woman's prospective on his act.

'So, you liked my act,' he said as he sat the drink in front of her.

'Yes. So many acts don't want to talk about sex nowadays. I mean it's not as if we aren't all at it. I have a confession to make. You know you said about Stand-Up groupies, well I am one.'

'Seriously?'

'Yes. I hope you are going to come back to my place and screw me into ecstasy.'

Jimmy smiled then looked round the bar to see who she was with. This must be a set up he thought. Nobody seemed to be bothered with what they were up to so he decided, for the moment, to go along with it.

'So, who are you here with tonight?' he asked.

'I am on my own. None of my friends are into comedy like me. Or comedians.'

Jimmy started to get nervous. If she was on the level, would he be up to the task she wanted him for. He gulped some of his drink down. She seemed genuine but he hadn't been, he just put the last bit in about groupies for a laugh. He wasn't laughing now. But he could be.

'So, what was your favourite joke?'

'The last one, about your mother and her teacher.'

'That wasn't a joke. It really happened.'

'Get away, really?' The girl went quiet.

'I take it the offer is off the table now, you know, the sex. Now that you know I am an old granny shagger?'

'No,' she said, with no conviction.

'No, I am only kidding. None of it happened. Although I am a school crossing patrol.'

'Really.'

They finished their drinks. 'Want another?'

'No, think we should head back to mine. If you are up for it?'

'Up for it? I was born up for it.'

They walked arm in arm to the bus stop. Emma lived in the city centre and it was a short bus run out to her flat. On the bus, Emma told the driver where they were heading while Jimmy paid.

'Four pound,' the driver said.

Jimmy handed him a tenner and two tickets dropped down. He waited for his change. When he asked, the driver pointed to a sign that said, correct change only.

'Robbing bastards,' he said to the driver who just smiled at him. 'Dick fucking Turpin,' he said before walking up the bus to join Em. He just hoped the journey would be worth it.

At her flat, Emma took him by the hand and led him straight through the unlit flat to the bedroom. She put a lamp on then took a small tin from a bedside cabinet. The white powder in it was put on her finger and rubbed on her gums.

'Want some?'

'What is it?'

'Breath freshener.'

Jimmy thought about it. Well, there would hopefully be a bit of kissing so he took some. Funnily there was no minty taste or in fact any strong flavour to it.

As soon as they were naked they were wrestling about on the bed. Karen, who was now his ex, was strictly sex under the covers and the missionary position. Fuck, she even kept her bra on.

Emma was the opposite and straight to business. She went down on him, sucking so hard on his penis that he thought she was going to loosen the fillings in his teeth. She knew how to pleasure a guy that was for sure. Jimmy was taken to levels of sexual fulfilment he had never even imagined before.

After Jimmy had orgasmed 3 times, he couldn't believe his body was still craving more.

'Need the toilet,' Emma said, leaving the bed. She went through to the toilet that was off the bedroom. Sitting on the pan, she had the door open and while doing a Number 2 promised Jimmy she would be lubed up for anal.

Jimmy laughed. Anal. He had always thought anal was wrong but he had never been offered it before. Now, what the fuck? Then he reached into the drawer and took the tin out again and rubbed some more powder into his gums. He was ready for anything Emma wanted. His prowess was surprising even him.

Jimmy woke and checked his phone on the floor. Just after 6am. It took him a few seconds to realise he was sweating like Susan Boyle in a cake shop. Emma was snoring in the bed next to him. His hands were now starting to shake. The one thing he knew was he had to get out of there before Emma woke up. She would be demanding another pounding and Jimmy was not up to it. He had to get back to the station and get back for his morning patrol. Picking his clothes up, he tiptoed out of the bedroom.

Clothed, he sneaked out the front door. The biting January wind made him shiver like a jakey's dog doing a shit. Walking fast would, he hoped, help getting his temperature back up. A 100 yards down the road, a lamppost stopped him from falling down.

A van drew up beside him. Turning, he saw it was a police van. The passenger's window slid down.

'Are you okay, sir?'

'No, I feel like shit.'

'Where are you going?'

'Central station.'

'Going the long way? It's the opposite way. Where are you coming from?'

'I was at a girl's last night. Emma, but I didn't get her second name.'

'Supertramp.'

'What?'

'She is one of the local prostitutes, our nickname for her is Supertramp. Quality though, we never hear anybody complaining.'

Jimmy suddenly felt flushed again. The shaking stopped and sweating started again.

The cops talked to each other then one told him to get in the back of the van.

'What! Are you arresting me.'

'No, son, community policing. We will take you to the station, the railway station.'

Jimmy looked at them warily. However the state he was in he didn't think he could make it to the end of the street he was on, much less to the station.

'So, you never said, was Supertramp worth the money?'

'Money? She never charged me. Turns out she is a Stand-Up groupie. I was doing Stand-Up last night and she, well, picked me up afterwards.'

The coppers laughed. 'I think you should check your wallet.'

Jimmy quickly pulled out his wallet. It wasn't as full as it had been last night.

'A £110. Fuck me.'

'Oh, I think she did. That's her going rate, £100 and a tenner for the Ecstasy.'

'Ecstasy! She told me it was breath freshener.'

The two cops howled with laughter.

'You ain't from the City, son?' Jimmy shook his head embarrassedly. 'Think you have learned a few lessons tonight.'

He sat there thinking he had. Then it dawned on him, she had never kissed him. Was that not the tell-tale about prostitutes? Boy, he had really been a sap. He believed his own hype, that somebody would like him because he was funny. What a fucking idiot he had been. There again he was one sexually pleased idiot.

On the train home, Jimmy stared at his phone. It was too early to call Karen. After last night, he questioned whether he did really want to get back with Karen with her boring sex. Last night had opened his mind, and a few orifices to better and different sex. Where to get another girlfriend?   There was nobody in the town where he lived that he fancied or more to the point any that fancied him. A dating agency, that could be the answer, widen his horizons.

Free dating agencies. The internet popped up with Kissing Frogs. It's free, he thought to himself, why not? So, the rest of the journey he spent putting in his details. Strike while the irons hot, he thought. He was entering a new chapter in his life, he felt. His life seemed to be changing so much, taking him in different directions.

Jimmy had never been so glad to see his bed again. He had done his morning stint at the crossing patrol then walked, slowly, back home. He woke with a start, he didn't know how long he had slept. Had he slept through his next stint? He found his phone in his jeans pocket. It was just after 11. Relief. Then he saw he had 6 contacts. Girls, all wanting to date him. Result!

He laughed as he thought it wouldn't just be his comedy that would be standing up for the next while. Another thought came to him as he lay in bed before he got up. That was when his jokes came to him. The latest drug taking in Yorkshire is EE by gum. Thank you Emma, he thought.

Rose. Jimmy was in the train to Glasgow again. He was meeting Rose beneath the clock in the Central Station. As he stepped off the train he was more nervous than he had been before his Stand-Up debut.

The guy in front of him was carrying a bouquet of flowers. Fucking wanker Jimmy thought, then wondered whether he should have brought something himself. Maybe not a big statement like that but a single rose or a box of chocs. Roses. God, why hadn't he thought of it earlier.

Sure enough bouquet guy was meeting a girl beneath the clock. There was only one girl there, was he going to nick Rose from him. No, as he got closer he could see this girl was in fact a woman probably in her 40's. Bouquet guy went down on a knee and produced a ring.

Oh my God, an actual proposal before his very eyes. Jimmy swallowed, how romantic.

Jimmy looked around, nobody else seemed to notice the drama unfolding in front of him.

Far from being overjoyed, the woman was overwhelmed and turned and walked quickly away. Bouquet guy stayed on his knee watching his intended storm off before getting up and going after her.

Jimmy continued to watch as the chase was on. He wanted to follow and see how the drama unfolded. Looking around, there was no sign of Rose. The time on his phone said 7:27. Three minutes, he ran off in the direction of the fleeing woman and her distraught suitor. The exit led to the taxi rank.

Jimmy got there in time to see the guy jump in the back of a taxi.

He could imagine him- follow that taxi. The driver- right gov, before chasing the hackney in front of him. Although he would know not to be too quick, he didn't want to lose his place in the rank for a couple of quid.

Jimmy waited until he saw the chasing taxi disappear out of sight. When he turned to go back beneath the clock, he spied in the nearest waste bin the bouquet of flowers.

Waste not, want not, he thought as he retrieved them. Looking in, he saw it was 6 red roses. This should be worth at least a blow job, he thought.

Back at the clock, still no sign of his date. He hoped the flowers didn't end up in another bin on the way home if she had shot him a dizzy. At the same time he wondered if the second taxi managed to catch the first. Maybe she was married. Living a secret life with her lover, just a bit of fun but he wanted to go further, somewhere she couldn't go. That was his theory.

His train of thought was interrupted by a tap on his shoulder.

'Rose!' Standing behind him was a version of a girl. Pretty looking and small. Nice figure and tiny. Nicely made-up, neat hair and petite. That was the word he had been looking for-petite.

'Jimmy. Is it Jimmy you prefer?'

'Yes. I take it you prefer Rose.'

They stood looking at each other for a few moments.

'Are those for me?'

'Yes, roses for a Rose.'

'Oh, they are lovely. A bit much for a first date. So, where do you want to go?'

'The thing is, I don't know any of the pubs round here. I only know the comedy clubs.'

'There is a nice wee pub down the street.'

Rose linked her arm around Jimmy's and marched him down the stairs and out of the station, proudly carrying her flowers.

The first two pubs were filled with Friday night revellers, very raucous, not the atmosphere they sought.

Round the corner was The Rower's Arms. It was quieter than the others. There was a bouncer on the front door.

'Do you think he is a chucker-inner? Don't see folk fighting to get in.'

Rose laughed. Jimmy liked that, first you get them laughing then you get their knickers off. That was the plan anyway.

The Neanderthal bouncer, looked down at them with disdain.

'What age are you?'

'Twenty three.'

'Not you, the dwarf.'

Rose thrust her ID in front of him. 'Don't know if you can read mate, but that's a driving licence.'

Jimmy realised she was angry and tried to help her by doing an impression of somebody steering. 'Peep, peep. Car,' he said sarcastically.

The guy was absolutely stone-faced. He glimpsed down at the plastic then moved aside to let them in.

'Thanks,' Rose said sarcastically.

After they went in, Jimmy asked, 'Maybe we should go somewhere else.'

'No, we can't let thugs like that waste our night.'

'Big thick gorillas like that bug me. Give them a bit of power and they abuse it.'

'Still, you were taking a chance. He could have cracked you one.'

'Probably saving it for the way out.'

They managed to grab a quiet table in the back. Jimmy got the drinks in. Lager for him, pink gin for her.

'Do you think the pub is named after Rowers as in rowing a boat or Rowers as in having a row, you know, him and her, Mr and Mrs coming to the pub and ending up fighting?'

'Have you not got a good image of Glasgow people?'

'What, no! I love them. I did my first gig last Monday and

it was great.'

'So, do you think you could make a career out of comedy?'

'God, I hope so. Don't want to be a lollipop man for ever.'

'Is that what you are?'

'Yes, that's my daytime job. Keeps me off the street.'

Rose laughed gently. 'Hope your Stand-Up is better than that.'

'Oh, it's a bit coarser. What do you do?'

'I'm a bouncer in Legoland.'

Jimmy's face was a picture. 'Really?'

'No, you daftie. I work as a salesgirl in the Lingerie Department in Debenhams.'

'Nice. And do you get a discount?'

'We get a discount on everything. So, what I spend it on, well it will be a while before you get to see that.'

Their drinks were finished. Rose insisted on getting the next round. When she came back with the drinks, Jimmy nipped into the toilet.

Jimmy returned to find Rose with a huge smile on her face.

'What?'

'Well, I know we just met but I think we could be perfect together.'

Jimmy was getting worried and more worried by the second.

'I mean I watch all those Married at First Sight programmes on the telly but I never thought it would happen to me.'

Was Rose suddenly one of those loony types who you said you liked them and they took this as a marriage proposal?

'I found your note in the roses.'

She handed him the small card that he hadn't seen in the flowers. It said simply- Will you marry me? Jimmy's mouth fell open. Did this mean he had to marry her? Did words on a card constitute a contract? Would it be so bad to marry her? So many things were buzzing about in his head. He turned to check Rose's reaction only to find her in tears from laughing.

'I don't know where you got the flowers from but at least it wasn't the cemetery.'

She got him, hook, line and sinker. Nothing for it but to confess. So he told her the whole story and if she had been there a few minutes earlier she would have witnessed it too.

Rose's eyes were wide with amazement at the story.

'So, what do you think happened next?'

'Oh, I know what happened. I lifted the flowers out of the bin and gave them to the most gorgeous girl I met beneath the station clock.'

'No, with the couple, silly.'

'I think she was married and was enjoying an affair with the guy. He misread the signals and wanted to marry her. What do you think? What would make you run away from a proposal?'

'Well, I didn't run away when I got your card.'

'What did you think when you first read the card then? Did you consider it?'

Rose blushed making her pretty cheeks even prettier, if that was possible.

'I thought you must have bought them cheap off some-body.'

'You didn't answer the second question.'

'That answer is for another day.'

Jimmy's phone pinged. He had set his phone with differ-ent ringtones for each caller

'Oh, that's my agent. You don't mind if I check it?'

'No. It could be your big break.'

Jimmy read his text. 'You beauty.'

'Good news?'

'Yes. The Laughing Chandelier, that's the place I did my first paying gig last Monday.
Well, they want me back on Monday. Better text him back. You should come, I can get you a free ticket.'

'No, not on a work night. I need 8 hours sleep or I am a mess the next day.'

'You could never be a mess in my eyes.'

'Charmer.'

'Why don't you get a microwave bed?'

'What's that?'

'They are great, you get 8 hours sleep in 20 minutes.'

Rose thought for a moment then laughed.

'Are you ever serious?'

'Yes.'

Jimmy leaned forward, so did Rose and they kissed.

Jimmy looked from the train window at the world speeding past. He had been nervous since he woke that morning. He reckoned this was worse than the previous week and his first gig.

He wished Rose was coming to see him but when she said she wasn't, well he had put in a few funnies about her, her height or rather lack of it. Still, he had arranged to meet her again on the following Saturday night.

Walking through the station he looked over towards the big clock. Nobody waiting for a date, no proposals. He still wondered how Friday's drama ended. His night ended with a snogging session in a shop doorway. Snogging with a hint of something more on offer the following week.

Going on stage was easier this time. As he got on stage he looked around the front row. Some folk seemed familiar, probably seen them at other gigs he had been at himself, sitting amongst them, wishing it was him up there. He had written a complete new set for the night. So many Stand-Ups were lazy. Wrote their 10, 15 minutes of material then used it so often they knew every word off pat. Many folk would go to the same club on the same night each week. They didn't want to hear the same patter.

'Evening Ladies, Gents and all other denominations. Right, a wee girl goes to stay with her gran for the first time. Getting ready for bed they go in the bathroom and brush their teeth. Oh, the gran says, you can help me, put my suppository in. The granny then wheeches up her goony. Gran, says the wee girl, do I put it in the brown dot or feed it to the turkey.'

Killed it, he thought. He loved it when there was a few seconds while the joke sank in then howls of laughter. Drink of water.

'I come from a big family but we never call each other by our names, we all go by our nicknames. My mother is a wee woman so we call her mini, short for mini-mum. My dad is the Genie, he always seems to appear when a bottle is opened. My sister is wee and fat and lads, we all know how easy it is to get a fat bird into bed. Yip, a piece of cake. Only in her case it would be a cake so we call her Shortcake. My brother is called the Gas Man because he has serviced a lot of old boilers in his day.'

Pause for a drink of water. Some are going okay, others are groaned at. From experience people will take one or two jokes away with them to tell friends. Throw enough at them and some will stick.

'My cousin Brian lost an eye in an accident, we call him Bran. My cousin Ann is very flat chested, so flat she has no knockers at all so we call her Doorbell. Cousin Frank is called Bung, short for Bungalow. He thinks it's because he is short and squat but it's because he is like a bungalow, fuck all upstairs.'

'Me, I have had a few nicknames over the years but my latest is Battersea, as in the dog home, on account of the number of dogs I've taken home over the years. And I don't mean 4 legged ones.'

Another drink before he changed the subject a bit.

'Well to better myself I have joined a dating agency. First date on Friday and the girl who turned up was lovely but, well, short. We went in a pub for a meal and the waitress brought her over a colouring book and crayons. When I went to the bar for a pint, the barmaid looked over to my table and said I thought you had started on the halves.'

This wasn't going as well as he had hoped. There were no laughs coming

'Still, at the end of the night she was the ideal height for something.' He then mimicked holding her head at his waist for a blowjob then patting an invisible head. There was a bit of laughing but then somebody shouted something from the back of the audience then a couple of people left, storming out noisily.

Jimmy caught a glimpse of them and it looked like one was a petite person. He got a horrible feeling in the pit of his stomach that it was Rose and a friend.

Still the show had to go on and he needed to get the crowd on his side with a belter of a joke.

'A guy goes into a library and asks if they have the new book about having sex with a small penis. The librarian says it's not in yet and he says that's the one.'

Finally a laugh. Drink of water then onto the next one.

'Right question for the guys, has a girl has ever given you a tug. You know a bit of hand relief. You know, oh, it's my monthly's, we can't have sex but I will relieve you.'

There was a bit of shouting out, mainly from guys that were with mates, not partners or girlfriends.

'What I have found is that girls either want to pull the skin off it or are afraid to touch it. I was at the pictures once and the girl I was with couldn't keep her tongue out of my ear. It was like an ear bath I was getting. She then rubbed my groin then asked if I wanted relief. So next thing she has my wee fellow out and starts rubbing it but she is afraid to touch the blooming thing.'

'Eventually I said give me it and I finished it myself. Now she was a bit peeved but when I asked to change seats so she could clean the other ear she stormed out. It was a bummer, she took the pick and mix with her.'

Jimmy finished the show and got good applause. As he left the stage an impending feeling of dread filled him, something told him Rose had been in the audience. As he headed through to the bar, he hoped if Rose had been in the audience she had left the building. No such luck. Sitting at the back of the bar, Rose was at a table with a bigger girl. From the other side of the bar Jim could see a family resemblance. Sister? Obviously a big sister. Taking the bull by the horns, he walked over to them.

'Can I get you two drink?'

'I will have a pint of fruit cider and Petunia will have a double vodka and coke.'

'Go gentle with the coke,' Petunia ordered. From her tone, she was not happy. Not happy at all.

Jimmy stifled a laugh, he was sure Petunia wouldn't be gentle with a man's coke.

Waiting at the bar to get served he could feel 4 eyes on him. He sneaked a glance in the mirror behind the bar and found the two girls staring daggers at him. It was going to take more than a drink to placate these two.

Jimmy sat the drinks down and his own pint.

'I told you to tell me if you were coming tonight, I would have got you free passes.'

Rose's voice started to tremble as she spoke. 'I wanted to surprise you.'

'But you surprised her, making her the butt of your jokes,' Petunia added.

'It's only jokes. We know they are not true. If you had told me you were coming I wouldn't have put that bit in.'

'Would it have been any different if she hadn't been here? You are still ridiculing her.'

'I wasn't. It was just after being with you those jokes came to me.' He tried to argue but it sounded lame even to him.

Jimmy thought he could have got on Rose's good side but Petunia, well, she didn't seem to have one.

Any chance of an amicable settlement was ruined when a couple of guys were leaving and one shouted over- Jimmy, loved the dwarf jokes. Jimmy gave the guy a thumbs up. Talk about lighting the blue touch paper. Petunia walked round behind Jimmy and grabbed the lapels of his jacket from behind. She pulled the jacket down so far, Jimmy couldn't move, he was trapped in his seat by the material. Rose then got up and splashed the remains of her drink into his face. She then grabbed the top of his trousers and poured the rest of his drink down into his pants. She followed it by a right fist, bang- right into the bread basket. Jimmy swallowed hard as the pain surged through him.

Who hit him, he wasn't too sure because he kept his eyes tight shut. This was followed by such a hard slap on his right cheek that he was sure it was Petunia's turn to abuse him.

After a few moments he opened his eyes which were a blur, filled with tears as well as sticky cider. Thankfully the two women had left. Struggling, he managed to get his jacket back on correctly. He took water from the water bottle in his pocket and put some in his hand to clear his face. He then walked to the toilet, the stiff legged walk you get when you piss yourself. The soaking wet trousers chaffing as he went. Even his socks were wet.

In the toilet he tried to tidy himself up but apart from drying the excess drink off with toilet paper, he still had sodden pants.

Back home, the house was in darkness. He lived with his mum and dad, the other siblings having flown the coop years ago. Late or not, he needed a bath. His legs were now all red and raw as the biting January wind had played havoc with the wet denim against his soft skin.

He ran the bath as quietly as he could.

'Oh, you are back. What's wrong, no prostitute tonight?' Jimmy's mother was outside the toilet door whispering in. Jimmy was absolutely mortified. He had told nobody, not a single person knew of his assignation the previous week. Except Emma and the two coppers, none of which would know his mother, who lived more than 15 miles away.

Wrapping a towel round his waist he opened the door.

'How did you know about that?'

'It was in your notebook. If you leave things lying about then you can't expect me not to read them.'

'Mum, that book is always with me. Except on Friday when I left it at the bottom of my sock drawer.'

'That's right. I was putting your socks in the drawer and I found it. The thing is everybody says its terrible that you need to go to well one of them.'

'Everybody! Who is everybody?'

'Just my friends. And Karen says she is disgusted. Glad she dumped you.'

'Karen. What are you telling her for? Anyway, it's not a diary. It's notes for my comedy. It's made up.'

'Oh, so all of a sudden you have an imagination. I don't think so. You've never had one before.'

Raging, Jimmy retreated to the bathroom. As he lay soaking in his bath one thing was for sure, he needed out from under his mother's poke nose.

Friday and Jimmy was on the train again. Paisley this time and the lovely Pamela. Pam was a redhead. Their reputation for being fiery hotheads and having a temper to match was enough to keep him away from them. Pamela, however, seemed different.

They met at the station. No clock there but she was waiting at the entrance way. Jimmy smiled. Pamela was pretty. More than pretty, she was hot- red hot. Her hair was down to her shoulders and more dark red than bright ginger. His heart was thumping, hopefully she felt the same.

They were both wearing double denim, jeans and jacket. Jimmy had a white t-shirt whereas Pam had a low cut top that showed more than a hint of her ample cleavage.

He leaned in for a cuddle. She smelt of expensive perfume.

'So, what's the plan for tonight,' she asked.

'Well, I don't know Paisley. Where do you recommend?'

'Depends what you want? Karaoke, wine bar, cheap and nasty, pub with grub or a romantic diner.'

'The romantic diner sounds great.'

Pamela burst out laughing. 'You are in Paisley, not Narnia. There's nothing romantic about any of the pubs in Paisley. That was a joke.'

'Oh, are you a bit of a comedian? Maybe I can use some of your patter in my Stand-Up routine.'

'You do Stand-Up. Wow.'

'Is there a comedy club in Paisley?'

Pamela laughed again. Jimmy fancied her the first second he saw her but when she laughed, he fancied, no lusted after her, even more.

When she stopped laughing she told him what was funny. 'Comedy club? We don't need them, every second person you meet is a comedian.'

Pamela now led him back beneath the railway bridge and across the road to a pub. It was clean and noisy when they walked in the door but seemed homely.

Some wag shouted, 'Shut that fucking door, you are letting the Winter in.'

'Is that a traditional Paisley welcome?' Jimmy asked.

'Only if they like you. If they don't like you you get a Paisley kiss.'

'What's a Paisley kiss?'

'It's like a Glasgow kiss only we knee you in the balls as well.'

Jimmy laughed and had more than warmed to Pamela. They grabbed their drinks and looked for a table. The only one was beside an elderly couple. There was no room at the bar so Pamela asked if they could join them.

The guy was dressed in an ill fitting suit, whitish t-shirt and a tartan bonnet. His red nose showed he was no stranger to a spirit. The missus, if that was their relationship, was wearing a tracksuit that had more lumps and bumps than a sack of spuds. She had badly dyed purple hair and poorly applied make-up.

'You can join us if you get us a drink,' the old guy said.

'Charlie, shut your hole. Leave the couple alone. Sit down.'

'No, it's okay, what are you drinking?' Jimmy asked.

'Double whisky, pal,' the bonnet said.

'You will get a single and like it, Charlie, and I will have a can of Pils.'

Jimmy went to the bar while Pamela blethered with her new besties.

When Jimmy returned Pam looked slightly embarrassed.

Tracksuit spuds was holding court. 'I was just saying to your friend that I thought you were married or at least engaged. You look like a such a nice couple.'

'No, it's our first date. We have only just met.'

'She said that but I didn't believe her. Anyway, when you get married, make sure Charlie and Vera are on the guest list. Charlie, how many years are we married this June?'

'Too fucking many,' he growled.

'Thirty fucking seven. Can you believe that hen?'

'No, you don't look old enough, you must have been a child bride,' Pamela said.

'Fuck off. So, what age are you?'

'Twenty seven.'

'Away, I thought you were going to say twenty one. Any kids.'

'I have an 8 year old daughter.' Pamela looked sideways at Jimmy. This wasn't the way she wanted break it to him but she couldn't deny it.

A child. A single mum. Jimmy had never thought about either scenario. Now, in a pub in Paisley, on a first date, sitting with two strangers, he suddenly had to think about it. He didn't have much time because Charlie was pulling at his sleeve to get his attention.

'Jimmy, are you going to pump her tonight?'

Now this was done in a stage whisper. Pamela, Vera and a few drinkers at the next table clearly heard it. They could hear them giggling.

Before Jimmy could answer, Vera rebuked her man.

'Charlie, that's enough! Anyway, it's obvious he will pump her. Would you pump her?'

Charlie smiled lasciviously.

'Well you have more chance in doing me in trap 2 and you have no chance of that. Not with my piles.'

Jimmy and Pamela cringed and didn't know how to answer to this latest outburst. Pamela looked at Jimmy with the International- lets get out of here look.

Jimmy took a big swig of his beer. He was going to make their apologies for leaving when Pamela, having swallowed her drink, spoke up.

'Come on Jimmy. Our table is booked for 8.'

'Oh, is that the time?' He swallowed another mouthful and got up.

Charlie turned to Vera and gave another stage whisper. 'She is desperate for her hole.'

'No, Charlie, it's a first date, he will need to feed her first.'

Outside the bar and away from sight, the two of them burst out laughing.

'God oh! It's true what you say, that's funnier than any Comedy Club I've ever been at.'

They continued along the street away from the pub laughing as they went. When they stopped laughing Pamela started sobbing.

'Are you all right?'

'No. I wanted to tell you about Michelle once I got to know you better. When Vera asked about having any children, I had to tell the truth. After all the trouble I had with her, I would never deny having her.'

Jimmy kept quiet because he didn't really know what to say.

'Here, give me a cuddle,' he said and for a few minutes they just clung to each other.

Emma wiped away the tears then turned to face him.

'Do you want to end the date here? I will understand?'

'What? No. I am just getting to know you. When I first saw you I thought wow! You are attractive, have a great sense of humour and I want to know you better.'

'Why do we not get a carry-out and go back to mine. I will tell you all about me and my life. After I tell you, you can decide if you still want to see me.'

'Well, I will tell you about my life, maybe you won't want to see me again.'

The taxi stopped outside Pamela's house. Jimmy paid while Pam went ahead and opened the front door. It was a bit of a struggle for him with two bags of drink and snacks.

When Jimmy walked into the hallway it wasn't what he expected. It was clean, clinically clean. As he walked through he saw the rest of the house was the same.

The main wall in the lounge was dominated by a huge print of Pamela and a girl who was obviously her daughter. They were cuddling and smiling, so happy and loving.

'That's amazing, the picture of you two.'

Pamela's smile filled her face.

'You know, you are really beautiful when you smile.'

'You just want to get into my pants.'

'Well, I've never been into cross dressing but I don't think your pants would fit me.'

'Always the comedian.'

'I wasn't being funny when I said you look beautiful.'

'Right, lets get a drink. You might not think I am so nice when I tell you my story.'

Pamela had been getting glasses and plates out. She took the drink bag off Jimmy and put the contents into the fridge, except of course something to drink right away.

Pamela caught Jimmy looking around.

'Spotless. Bet you think I have one of those cleaning phobia's.'

'Well, it had crossed my mind.'

'Michelle doesn't keep well. She is very susceptible to germs and the place needs to be like this all the time.'

They sat on the sofa together, facing the family print.

'She looks healthy in the picture.'

'Oh, she has good spells and bad ones. Right, before I tell you about me, I want you to know anytime you want to go, just walk out. No hard feelings.'

Jimmy nodded but feared for the worst, what could be so bad?

'So, when I said Michelle was 8, she is nearly 12. I am 27, I had her when I was 16. At the time I was on drugs. Hard drugs. Wait. I will go back a bit. I was clever, good at school, I even won prizes. Then, when my mum died I went off the rails. Started drinking, then fell in with the wrong crowd. Missed school, then got suspended. Went from drink to drugs then started going with Raymond. Ray was 19, had money, came from a good family, posh house and everything. Next thing, I got pregnant. I would love to say that as soon as I was pregnant I stopped the drugs but I didn't. That is the reason Michelle is the way she is. Every day I feel guilty for what I have done to her.'

Tears ran down Pamela's cheeks. Jimmy swallowed hard, it wasn't easy listening.

'Somehow I survived the first year with her. God knows how. His family didn't help. I was the bad influence to their Raymond. He was their Golden Boy who could do no wrong. Then he overdosed. He was at a mates house and next thing I get a knock on the door and that was it. Never touched drugs again. Never even had alcohol until last year when I started dating.'

'So, hows that been?'

'First few dates I didn't drink at all but I was a bundle of nerves. So I take a drink just to settle my nerves. Dating has not been great. I've not managed a second date.'

'Why?'

'Mention a girl with a disability or special needs, whatever way you want to put it and you can't see guys for dust.'

Pamela got up and stood in front of the picture, staring at her daughter's image.

'I would never give her up for a man.'

'Their loss, I think.'

'Thanks.'

'So, you haven't said, where is Michelle tonight?'

'Oh, I drug her with sleeping pills then lock her in her bedroom. She will be out cold until the morning.'

Jimmy was flabbergasted. In fact his flabber had never been so gasted. Then Pamela laughed. 'Your face. Your face was a picture.'

'Well, you are right about what you said earlier, every second person in Paisley is a comedian. God, you had me going. So where is she?'

'She is staying the night with the in-laws. They have mellowed over the years. She is their blood after all. They treat her like the Princess she is now.'

'So, I think I will need to tell all about my life. I was like you in Primary school, very smart, always in the Top 10. Then, when I hit puberty, I got lumps in my chest. Imagine a 13 year old boy with small boobs. Now the boys night not notice but I felt they were huge, of Page 3 standard. So, I went to the Doctors and was sent to the hospital. The specialist there said it was just excess fat caused by my hormones changing my body, said they would dissolve through time. That did nothing to help my self-consciousness. I became very shy. So shy when I was in 3rd year they mixed up my options. Now anybody else would have went to the teachers about it. Me? No, I was just so shy I just took the subjects I was given. I ended up doing Woodwork, I fucking hated Woodwork, wanted to do Techy Drawing. So one day I decided I had to change and became my alter ego. A happy go lucky, always joking character. Class clown. So the result was, I left school with no qualifications. I drifted from dead end job to dead end job. I was laid off time after time, too much carry on in my head. So I ended up unemployed and spent all my time watching comedians on TV.

Two years ago I got a job doing the School Crossing Patrol then last year I did a Stand-Up course at College and it gave me the confidence to perform. I have done a lot of open mike nights and now I have an agent and am doing gigs.'

'School crossing?'

'The bru were going to stop my money so I had to do it or lose my money. It suits me, three spells a day and never have to work nights or weekends.'

'What about girls?'

'I had a few girlfriends, the last one was Karen. We were together for 3 years and she wanted us to get engaged and me to give up the comedy. Wouldn't come and see me, then she dumped me by text.'

'That's shocking.'

'So, joined the dating agency and here I am.'

'Here you are. So, how is it since you and Karen were, eh intimate?'

'Three months.'

'It's been over six months since I had any action.

'Well, come over here and lets get intimate.'

Pamela joined Jimmy on the sofa and they embraced. The kissing was hot and the fondling got raunchier by the minute.

After 15 minutes Pamela whispered in his ear. 'Do you want to take this upstairs?'   'What the sofa? Have you not got a bed?'

'You better not be so funny in bed.'

Pamela raced up the stairs and Jimmy followed.

'Have you got a condom? You aren't going bareback.'

 'I've got one in my wallet for emergencies.'

'One? Good job I've some, for emergencies.'

Pamela then proceeded to strip off. Jimmy was amazed at how white her skin was. Especially when it contrasted with her dark red hair. She was slim and had smallish breasts when her Wonderbra came off but her nipples surprisingly big in comparison. She slipped off her trousers and pants. Above what would have been her panty line was a small scar, obviously from a Cesarian. She was shaven and had no pubic hair.

Jimmy pulled off his t-shirt and displayed a small pot belly. The boobs were still there although they would pass easily as moobs now. Dropping his trousers his erection was standing up proudly.

He rolled on the rubber he had stashed in his pocket earlier. Pamela was lying on the bed waiting on him. He kissed her and ran his hands over her erect nipples.

'Be gentle,' she pleaded.

He lay on top and pushed himself in as gently as he could.

Afterwards they lay together on the bed.

'So, the million dollar question is, do you want to see me again?'

Jimmy laughed. 'I was going to ask you the same question but was afraid to.'

'Why?'

'In case you said no. Did my man boobs not scare you off?'

'No. They are quite cute really. Now, I don't want you to think I am kicking you out but I can't let you stay the night. If Michelle and the in-laws turn up and a strange man is here, what will they think?'

'No, I can understand it. Can you call me a taxi?'

'You're a taxi.'

'I asked for that.'

Jimmy was on the train to Paisley again. They had another date a fortnight later. This time they went for a meal and drinks then back to hers, Jimmy catching the last train home.

Before he left Pamela dropped a bombshell, her in-laws were on holiday for a month so couldn't keep Michelle. Jimmy couldn't bear to be away from Pamela for that long so he suggested he come over on the Saturday and meet Michelle. This was a big day and he hoped it went well. Over and over he had said to Pamela what if she didn't like him but she told him to just be himself, treat Michelle the way he would treat any other 12 year old. Only thing was, the only contact he had with 12 year olds was to help them across the road.

Pamela and Michelle were waiting outside the station. Michelle was using her walking frame and greeted Jimmy with a smile.

'Mum said you were nice but didn't say you were this nice.

Might even fancy you myself.'

Jimmy laughed. 'No wonder there are no comedy clubs in Paisley, eh.'

Ice broken, they had a lovely day, going round the shops, eating at McDonalds then a special taxi home.

Pamela bathed Michelle and got her dressed for bed.

'Jimmy, Michelle has a treat for you. When she heard you did Stand-Up, she decided she would tell you a few jokes.

'Oh, right. Do you want me to introduce her?'

Michelle nodded.

'Lady and Gentleman, all the way from Paisley in Scotland, put your hands together for Michelle.'

Jimmy and Pamela applaud her.

'Right, there was a man with no arms and no legs at the bus stop. The bus stops and the doors open and the driver says-how are you getting on?'

Jimmy looks at Pamela with the kind of look Simon Cowell has when, on the few occasions somebody on Britian's Got Talent actually got some talent.

'A lady advertises for a man who won't run away from her, won't hit her and will love her. So her doorbell rings and there is the man from the bus earlier. So he says I am the man for you. I have no legs so I cannot run away. I have no arms so I cannot hit you. But, said the woman, you cannot love me. Well, he said, I rang the doorbell didn't I.'

Jimmy and Pamela start to clap.

'One more,' Michelle said. 'What do you call a man with no arms and legs in the swimming pool? Don't know- Bob.'

This time Jimmy and Pamela stand up and clap. Michelle takes a bow.

'That's brilliant. But why do all your involve a man with no arms and no legs?'

'Well, a man like that couldn't really exist so I wasn't making a fool of somebody.'

'Is that what you think we do? I don't make a fool of anybody. Except myself.'

'Maybe your different from the other guys on the telly.'

'I am. And if I get on the telly, I won't change.'

'Chelle, tell Jimmy where you are going on Monday.'

'I am off on my holidays.'

'Oh, where too?'

'Loch Lomond.'

'That sounds great.'

'Right young lady, time for bed.'

'Right mum. Night Jimmy. See you in the morning.'

Pamela took her daughter to bed while Jimmy wrote her jokes in his notebook.

Pamela returned and grabbed Jimmy on the face. She kissed him.

'Well, you made a big impression. She really likes you.'

'So, where is she off to on Monday?'

'Respite care. A charity takes her from Monday to Friday to give me a break. It's a lovely place in the country. They had a call off so she got the chance and wants to go. So, I will have the house to myself if you fancy a sleepover.'

'What about Monday?. I am doing Stand-Up again on Monday. How about you come with me to Glasgow then back here after. I can put a holiday in for Tuesday and we can spend the day together.'

'No, Monday's out for me. Tuesday's good. Put a holiday in for the Wednesday and we could even stay in bed all day.'

'Sounds dreamy.'

Train again. Monday night and for once there were no nerves. Jimmy had, he felt, his best script to date. That was until his phone beeped. His agent usually emailed so a text was special.   'Talent scout watching tonight. Usual top performance will do it.'

He got his book out again, reading and rereading his script, as he called it, all the way to Glasgow. Through the station and he couldn't even look to the clock in case it deflected his focus.

Instead of the usual beer to steady his nerves he stuck to water. All too soon he had the microphone in his hand.

'Ladies and Gents, I recently met a disabled girl who had me in tears with her Stand-Up.'

He then proceeded to tell them her jokes. Smashed it. He followed it with some of his own pearlers, 'President Trump swallowed 2 Viagra, he got taller.'

He paused for effect. 'Jonathon Ross' wife said to him every time you speak to me I get wet. Do I turn you on, he asked. No, you spray when you talk.'

Jimmy paused for a water break. It was going great, they were laughing at everything, he had them in the palm of his hand.

'I was walking home last week and I inadvertently walked down a street where prostitutes hang out. Three times I had to walk down it before I was propositioned. So I said how much do you charge? She said £30 for a blowjob, £100 for full sex. Well, I said I've only got £80. So I got the old fellah out and she looked at it and said, Jesus, can I loan you £20.'

Jimmy continued his act and got his first ever standing ovation when he finished.

Buzzing, he decided to forget about having a drink, he felt as if he was walking on air as he headed for the station. He was going to Paisley, he couldn't wait until the next night to see Pamela.

Settled on the train, it was just pulling out of the station when his phone rang. His agent.

'Jimmy. The best news, how do you fancy opening for Grappler on his upcoming tour.'

'Grappler? Is he not a wrestler?'

'He was a wrestler but has done some telly work and pod-casts. Now he has been signed up to do a Stand-Up tour. He is a big fan of yours and there is even talk of you being one of the writers for his material.'

'Full time comedy. Fancy it? You better believe I fancy it.'

'Right, I will email the details tomorrow. Okay, bye now.'

After he had rung off, Jimmy sat staring at his phone. Had that really happened? He checked his call list. Yip, his agent phoned him. Opening for Grappler. He wanted to phone Pamela, he knew she of all people would be really glad for him but he wanted to surprise her.

Jimmy leapt off the train and sprinted down the stairs and out into the street. He ran through to the taxi rank and jumped into the first cab. He sat back but couldn't relax. The 2 miles or so seemed like 20. Finally the cab stopped and Jimmy threw the driver a tenner.

The living room light was on. He knocked on the door, no reply. Looking in the living room window he saw Pamela on the sofa. She was asleep or unconscious. No response as he rattled on the window. Getting frantic, he tried the front door. Locked. He ran round the back door checking the windows as he went. All shut tight. The back door, he tried it and the handle dropped down. It wasn't locked.

'Pamela!' Jimmy shouted as he ran in.

Lying on the sofa Pamela was neither unconscious or asleep, she was doped up to her eyeballs. Jimmy felt sick to the pit of his stomach. There was a spoon and other drug paraphernalia on the coffee table. She had a belt round her arm.

'Pam! Pamela!' The only reaction was a slight opening of the eyes. Unseeing eyes, only the whites showing.

'I love you Pamela! Loved you. How could you do this?' he screamed.

His right fist was bunched. For a few seconds he was so angry he felt like punching her. Instead he fell to his knees in front of her, a broken man.

'You said you had stopped the drugs. I believed you. You lying cow!'

Tears streaming down his face, Jimmy got up and ran out the way he came in, through the back door. What a fucking sap he had been. I'm off the drugs, none since her ex died. Lies, lies, lies, he thought bitterly.

Jimmy kept running. Fast as he could, running in the direction he thought the station was. After a few hundred yards he could run no more. His chest was heaving, sweat blinded him then he was sick at the side of the road. What have you done to me junky?

A couple of cars passed then a taxi. Jimmy waved. The guy slowed and the passenger window slid down.

'Station mate.'

'Listen, pal, I'm private hire I can't stop in the street and pick you up. Phone the number and I will get you round the corner.'

'Tenner to the station asap.'

'Sorry, it's the rules.'

'Twenty.'

'Get in.'

The train journey passed quickly for Jimmy. His mind was all over the place. Best Stand Up he had ever done. On the verge of full time in comedy then Pamela. Fucking junky Pamela. The question that kept coming into his head, should he stand by Pamela. Help her get clean?

It would come into his head that they could work out her problems but then what if he was away on tour, what would she be doing? Any excuse and she would be injecting or snorting or whatever. No, he and Pamela were over. Then there was Michelle. What a special girl and he couldn't get to know her better. Michelle deserved better from her mother. Sure she had a hard life but drugs weren't the answer.

The train stopped. Only a few got off, Jimmy followed them up the platform and into the night. Would he get any sleep tonight, he wondered with all that had happened? Could he start thinking about the positives, new material was needed with his new career.

When he got to the end of the street he saw the living room light at his house was on. Half past eleven, his parents were never up at this time. Something was wrong. A death? Uncle Harry hadn't been well. Maybe one of them was sick.

Jimmy walked quickly up the avenue. There was noise coming from the house. Not arguing, raised voices and laughing.

The scene that awaited him was a scenario he could never have imagined. Mum and Karen were sitting on the couch drinking white wine. Dad was in his chair nursing a glass of whisky.

'What's going on?'

'We have been to Glasgow,' his mum piped up.

'Oh, so was I but I never saw you. It is a big place after all.'

'No, but we saw you.'

'What?'

'Yes,' Karen said. 'We were at your comedy show.'

'But you said that I was wasting my time with, what were your exact words? All that rubbish. Anyway, how did you know where I was?'

'You might not have listened to anything I ever said to you when we were going together but I listened to you.'

'So.'

'So what?'

'Did you like it?'

His mum piped up. 'Oh, you were brilliant son. My favourite was the guy who said this cucumber tastes fishy.'

'I liked the stuff about the guy with no arms or legs,' Karen said.

Mum, who was a bit tipsy started laughing. 'Fishy cucumber. We all know how it tasted fishy. I've never used a cucumber, I just use my vibrator.'

Jimmy looked around the room. Sure, it looked like the house he left that afternoon but now he seemed to be in Daliesque version of his life. A fourth or fifth dimension that looked like the same bricks and mortar but was inhabited by different versions of the people he had left earlier.

'Did you go dad?'

His father just smiled and showed him his glass.

'No, your father spent the evening in the company of Mr. Walker.'

'The old guy from down Drago Road?'

'No, Mister Johnny Walker.'

Dad just smiled and shook his glass gently, not daring to spill any.

'You better not have drunk too much. I'm after, what is it you say, Jimmy? A good pumping.'

Jimmy looked at Karen who just smiled, as if it was natural to hear his mother talk about having sex.

'I think I need a drink.'

'Get a glass, I will give you a wee dram.'

Jimmy couldn't believe that either, his father had never offered him a drink in his life. Not his special whisky.

Jimmy lifted a glass from the sideboard, all the time thinking how things couldn't get any weirder. His father filled his glass then emptied his own. He then urged his son closer, to listen while he whispered in his ear.

'Better get upstairs. She calls it our marital needs, I call it Enter the Dragon.' Father then chuckled to himself. Jimmy hoped he remembered that line, it was a belter.

Jimmy sat next to Karen and took a swig. It was the first time he had ever drank whisky and he could feel it burn all the way down his throat. No wonder the Red Indians called it firewater.

He then closed his eyes. Maybe it was some weird daydream, although he didn't know if you got them at night. He opened them to see his mother and father leave the room arm in arm. The only other time he had seen them in such close contact was in their Wedding photograph from 30 years ago.

Jimmy drank some more whisky then looked at Karen. She was staring at him.

'Do you know what I am going to tell you?'

'I don't know but after the night I have had nothing would surprise me.'

'I was wrong.'

That surprised him. A woman admitting she was wrong. He was definitely in some Twilight Zone.

'I was wrong to say your comedy stuff was stupid and a waste of time. I was wrong to dump you by text. In fact, I was wrong to split up with you.'

Jimmy let that hang in the air for a bit.

'I still love you. Since we split I must admit I have had sex with a few men. But, but all the time I was thinking of you. Wishing it was you.'

'A few.'

'It was nothing. It was just sex. I thought I was getting back at you but really I was getting back at myself. I still thought you were wasting your time with the Stand Up. That's why your mum and I went tonight. That was when I saw the Jimmy I fell in love with. You were alive on that stage. You were the guy that chased me to go out with you. That romanced me and stole my heart. I want to be with you now and forever.'

'Well, there is one thing.'

'You met somebody else?'

Things were whirling in his mind like a tornado. He was definitely over Pamela after tonight. At least he thought he was. No, he hoped he was. Deep down he knew he still felt deeply for Karen. Loved her? In a way but after his sexual awakenings since their split, well, how could he live with the Missionary position all his life.

'No, there is nobody else. But what if I was offered a tour. Away from home for weeks, maybe months. You would be thinking I was out looking for other women while I would probably be in digs working on other material.'

'We would find a way. I could come and visit. See your show. That's it. Would I still love you if you were famous? With comedian groupies after you, could I trust you? I think we would need to deal with that if it happened.'

'it's happened, I've been offered a tour.'

'No. Really. Who with?'

'Grappler.'

'Grappler, the wrestler. But you cannot wrestle.'

'He was a wrestler but he does other things. He has done telly stuff and podcasts and he is now set to do Stand-Up. I would be his opener, the guy who goes on before him and kind of gets the audience in the mood.'

'Will you be on the television?'

'I don't know but it's a foot on the ladder to a full time career in comedy.'

They were interrupted by raised voices from the room above, his parents bedroom.

'I want you to do that with me.'

'Argue?'

'They aren't arguing. They are fucking.'

Jimmy laughed. He had never heard Karen say the F word before and it sounded funny when she said it.

' Right now, I want you to strip off. Right here, right now. Love me like you have never loved me before. Ravage me, I want orgasms and multiple orgasms.'

She started peeling off her clothes.

'Would it not be more private up in my bedroom?'

By then she had her blouse and bra off. She cupped her breasts then thrust them towards him.

'Now!' she demanded.

Karen had always been protective of her breasts. Treated them like friends, her pet names were Ant and Dec. This was the first time Jimmy had seen them in the flesh.

Karen pulled him towards her chest and he kissed one. He hoped it was Ant, he hated Dec.

WHAT HAPPENS NEXT?

This book was written just before Lockdown   started.

Follow what happens next in ;

Every Hole is a Goal 2 : Lockdown Love.

The sequel will also follows the mis-adventures of 4 other love yearning Lotharios.

Follow Jimmy's adventures in Stand-Up School, The Class of 2019 the prequel to his   adventures in my previous book.

DISCLAIMER

As far as I know there is not a Dating App called Kissing Frogs. Surprisingly this is all   fiction. Any resemblance to any-body is accidental.

Made in United States
Troutdale, OR
12/20/2023

16280895R00106